Deadly Vestige

N.C. Lewis

Copyright © 2019 by N.C. Lewis

This is a work of fiction. The characters, organizations, and events portrayed in this novel are the product of the author's imagination or are used fictitiously, and any resemblance to actual persons, living or dead, businesses, companies or events, or locales is entirely coincidental.

All rights reserved. No part of this publication may be reproduced, distributed, or transmitted in any form or by any means, including photocopying, recording, or other electronic or mechanical methods, without the prior written permission of the author, except with brief quotations embodied in critical reviews and certain other non-commercial uses permitted by copyright law.

ALSO BY N.C. LEWIS – The Bagington Hall Mystery

SHADOWY SECRETS LURK beneath the surface of an idyllic Norfolk Country House...

THE BAGINGTON HALL MYSTERY

N.C. LEWIS[1]

Norfolk, England, 1923. Cromer is a sleepy village on the English coast. But things are about to liven up there, when Maggie Darling returns home from a seventeen year stint in London to work for her uncle's new maid service business.

No sooner has she arrived, when she gets mixed up in an agriculture strike, mistaken as a suffragette and loses a three legged kitten. But when a dead body shows up it all becomes very complicated...

---

1. https://books2read.com/u/3Ge7Wn

Grab your copy today![2]

ABOUT THE TOWN OF SKEGNESS

Skegness is a seaside town on the east coast of England, about one hundred and fifty miles from London. It is famous for its beach, offshore wind turbines...and enormous seagulls.

---

2. https://books2read.com/u/3Ge7Wn

Chapter 1

AN EIGHTY-YEAR-OLD boogied in a skimpy bikini, my feet hurt, and I was frantic.

The woman's name was Emily Johnson. She wore a wide-brimmed, pink sun hat, nothing on her feet, and shook everything there was to shake on her scrawny body.

With a week until the end of May bank holiday, the first wave of summer tourists crowded onto the sand: hundreds of pensioners and retired folk for the annual Retirees' Spring Festival.

A bright sun in the cloudless, blue sky warmed the sand. The entire country was in a mini heatwave. Beachgoers cast aside their winter cardigans, woolly jerseys, and bleak-coloured jackets. Bright colours covered the sand—pinks, purples, yellows, oranges, and lots of shirts, skirts, and towels, with pineapple patterns.

This group of scantily clad senior citizens were engaged in a mid-morning Zumba class. Two large speakers blasted Latin American beats. Forgetting my worries for a moment, I stared at Emily. She skipped and twirled, face upturned, arms spread wide. The woman reminded me of a person just set free after years in captivity. Or a crazy person moments before incarceration.

I couldn't tell which.

After a few more twirls, my eyes drifted to a large overhead banner:

GRAB YOUR LAST TANGO BEFORE SUNDOWN WITH US!

COME LIVE IN THE MONKSTHROPE RETIREMENT COMMUNITY.

A slender woman in her fifties at the front of the class moved like a Merengue dancer. She wore yoga pants and a baggy, bright-orange Monksthrope Retirement Community T-shirt and shuffled across the sand shimmying and shaking like a Bollywood dancer.

"Looking good, Emily," the class instructor said. "Girl, you're moving quicker than a woman half your age."

I let out a piggish snort then weaved through the bopping bodies, dodged wild arms, and stepped around twirling legs. The spritely group of grannies and grandads kept up a pace that put my middle-aged, unexercised body to shame.

The class instructor pointed in my direction. "Come join us."

Heads turned.

"Girl, you'll love it at Monksthrope," said a lady wearing a flowing, peach-coloured wrap around her waist. "We're a free-spirited senior community." Her strapless, pineapple-patterned top jiggled as she gyrated, exposing more than I wanted to see.

I moved to Skegness for a fresh start, a chance to reboot my life. Dancing barefoot in the sand with scantily clad retirees was not part of the package.

"Thank you, but no." I'd not been to the hamlet of Monksthrope and had no intention of visiting, either. "I live here. I'm a local, just out for my daily stroll."

Life in Skegness got off to a good start when I found a cheap place to live, made friends with an overfed cat named Mr Felix, and landed a full-time reporter position at the *Skegness Telegraph*.

The newspaper closed in my first week.

Things went downhill faster than a snowball in a blizzard after that.

And now, my only source of income—an overnight job frying doughnuts at Fantasy Gardens Amusement Arcade, is on hold. The local health and safety office closed the facility down. If it opens again, it won't be this summer season.

A puff of jaded air forced its way between my lips as I glanced towards the heavens. The sun beat down like the final demand from the taxman. My life reboot in Skegness was taking longer than I'd hoped.

I needed a job.

I needed money.

I was frantic.

And my feet hurt.

I'd forgotten about the Retirees' Spring Festival; otherwise, I would have avoided this stretch of beach. Tourists were good for the town, but they turned my daily stroll into a London rush-hour crawl.

I gazed past a group of retirees throwing a Frisbee to a row of benches lining a low wall beyond. That was my destination. This early in the season, most benches were empty. Next weekend, the seats would be full to overflowing with families from nearby towns. But today they were free. Well, except for a lone figure, feet swung up, lying horizontally on the centre bench.

"Mrs Cudlow!"

I spun around to see the sweating face of Constable Wriggly. A plump man in his early forties, he had a reputation for saying, "I'm off duty, Sergeant," or "It's not up to me; ask the person in charge."

"Constable, what a pleasant surprise," I said, pleased to recognise a familiar face.

He dabbed a handkerchief over his forehead, letting out a disgruntled mumble. "The inspector's got me back on the beat. Feels like I've been walking for miles and in all this bloody, awful heat. I don't do well in the sun."

I let out a sound I hoped was suitably sympathetic. "At least with the Retirees' Spring Festival in town everyone is in a good mood."

A large group of retired people, surrounded by a plume of smoke, shuffled by. They giggled, voices dropping to a low mumble as they walked by the police officer. There was a definite smell of marijuana in the air.

Constable Wriggly sighed, letting out a sound like the distant rumble of thunder on a late summer afternoon. "A man of my detective abilities shouldn't be plodding the beat. It's like asking Sherlock Holmes to sell ice cream. And now I'm supposed to be handing out business cards with my mobile phone number on them—community outreach."

I said, "Oh well, if it helps everyone feel safer."

He snorted. "Here take ten of the buggers, else I'll never shift 'em.'"

I took a small stack of cards from the officer, glanced at the top card, and smiled. "Very professional. At least I've got your number if ever I need it."

Again, he snorted. "This week, I've a few night shifts as well. It'll be hell in the nightclubs. Last year a group of pensioners got into a fight over the winner of the 1987 English Football Association Cup final. I don't know why I bother."

Again, I murmured a sympathetic sound.

The constable rubbed his chin. "When the pensioners arrive it's like spring break at Daytona Beach in Florida, only with seasoned professionals who've had a lifetime's practise misbehaving." His head turned, following the group of marijuana-smoking senior citizens, with flat eyes. "The beach has turned into a hippy commune just like that place outside of Bargoed in Wales."

"Perlysiau Village?" I'd read about the vegan community in an online article.

"That's it!" The constable's eyes narrowed. "Frankly, Mrs Cudlow, I didn't expect to see you amongst this lot." He made a grand sweeping gesture with his arms. "Most honest locals stay well clear of this part of the beach during the festivals. But you've not been in town long, I suppose."

To most locals, I was still an outsider, but I didn't feel like one. "Next year, I'll stay well clear."

"See you do that. Strange things happen during the Skegness festivals. If I were you, I'd keep off the beach until this one is over."

That got me curious. "What types of strange things?"

The constable's voice dropped an octave. "Must have been ten years ago, and I was a lot lighter on my feet when it happened." He stopped, eyes glancing across the sand to a line of food tents. "Is that Dee Dee's?"

Dee Dee's Famous Sausage Rolls were a favourite of the Skegness Police Department. I didn't know what it was about the crisp pastry creations, but one whiff was like blood to a mosquito to the constable.

He pulled a mobile phone out of his pocket. "Yep, it's eleven-thirty, time I had a little break. Got to get me a sample of Dee Dee's and take the weight off my feet. See you later and be safe."

"Before you go, why don't you tell me what happened ten years ago?" Curiosity is one of my weaknesses. Once it gets a grip, it won't let go.

Constable Wriggly glanced towards the tents then back. "I was on foot patrol at this very festival. The crowds were unusually heavy that year. You could barely move on the beach, and there was music playing. A giant party, like today." He looked towards the food tents. His body stiffened.

I followed his gaze. A line was forming outside of Dee Dee's.

"Please continue, Officer. Don't worry about the line. I'm sure you can walk straight to the front, given you are in uniform."

He relaxed. "Well, there was an I.A. Channer exhibition on at the Beachside Museum that year."

"The Skegness illustrator?" I'd seen drawings in the museum. They had a childlike quality.

"That's right." Constable Wriggly glanced towards Dee Dee's. "As the music played, it happened."

"What?"

"The Dancing Hands Mystery."

"Eh?"

"That's what the local press called it." The officer half closed his eyes as if drawing deep into a dark corner of his mind to recall the memory. "Fiona Fenchurch, a recently retired festival goer collapsed as she was dancing."

"Heart attack?"

"Strangled."

I stepped back a few steps, shock etched into my face. "Strangled?"

"Right here on the beach, in broad daylight, with thousands of people all around, and I was dancing... err... standing next to the victim!"

The journalist in me kicked in. "What happened?"

Constable Wriggly rubbed his chin. "I don't know."

There were a million things I wanted to ask, but I said, "There must have been lots of witnesses. What did they see?"

"That's the funny thing. I didn't see anything, nor did anyone else."

"But there were people all around, right? Someone must have seen something."

"Nothing." The constable wiped his forehead with the now moist handkerchief. "And that's not the worst of it."

"No?"

Again, Constable Wriggly dabbed at his forehead. "While I was standing guard waiting for the ambulance, the body disappeared."

"That's impossible! People don't get strangled on a crowded beach in broad daylight while dancing next to a police officer and then have their guarded body disappear."

"The case was never solved. I think it doomed my chances of making it to detective." Constable Wriggly half turned, gazing off into the distance as if recalling a distasteful memory. "They say Old Betty slayed the victim with her own hands then dragged the body into the sea."

A tingle of curiosity shot up my spine. "Who is Old Betty?"

The police officer blinked as if coming back to the present. "Like I say, stay off the beach. We don't want you to become one of the statistics, do we, Mrs Cudlow?"

Chapter 2

I WATCHED CONSTABLE Wriggly hurry away towards Dee Dee's and slipped off my sandals, placing them in my shoulder bag. That eased the ache in my feet a little. Then I glanced down at my hand, rubbing the finger that once held my wedding ring. Ten years married; five years divorced—no children. The separation was at my request, not his fault.

Toby, my ex has a heart as big as the Atlantic Ocean, a man who never gives up. No matter how bad things became, he was always a source of hope.

I closed my eyes for a second, memories making my throat dry. He'd been in touch.

We watched a show in Lincoln.

It was fun.

"Doris, I still love you, and I'll wait," Toby had said after the show. "But the clock is ticking; we don't have forever."

I continued to walk towards the bench, narrowly missing a pair of elderly ladies in tiny bikinis. A group of equally old men shambled goggle-eyed behind.

Life as a single woman in London doesn't come cheap, that's why I'd left the capital city. Skegness was my chance to make a fresh start, to pursue my dream to become a full-time newspaper reporter, and to heal.

With the closure of the *Skegness Telegraph* I knew the chances of landing another full-time journalist position were low. Everywhere in England there are hordes of unemployed reporters tossed overboard by the dying print industry. And every year a multitude of eager media studies students graduate from universities.

Then there was my age.

I was in my forties with only a handful of worthwhile articles to my name, mostly in print magazines I didn't read.

But I stayed in Skegness anyway.

Despite my lack of progress, I knew good things were about to happen. Life wouldn't take me down without a fight.

A song popular several decades ago blared over the speaker system. I felt a mass of people crowd around. Something cold and clammy gripped my arm and tugged. I glanced to my immediate right.

"Let's boogie, darling," said a plump man with ferret eyes, whose belly swelled over tight-fitting, Hawaiian-style bathing trunks. He looked to be in his seventies, but his hands were big and strong like they could squeeze things until they stopped moving.

"Hey!" I shouted, but the pulsating music drowned out my words. There was no escape from his iron-clad grip. His eyes were wild as we swung from side to side in beat to the once popular tune. At least, I thought, as we danced barefoot in the sand, there are so many people gyrating that if he attacked with those hands, there'd be witnesses.

The song ended.

Flushed and breathless my eyes darted wildly around for an escape route, but my feet hurt too much to run. I glimpsed Constable Wriggly in the distance at Dee Dee's Famous Sausage Rolls tent. He held a plate in his hand. I thought about screaming, but he was too far away to hear, neither was he the heroic police officer who comes running regardless of the danger. Anyway, with all the people around, I didn't want to be the centre of a big fuss.

"Got to go now," I said in a polite voice. "Thank you for the dance."

A warm breeze carrying the tang of saltwater swept in from the sea. The sun dipped momentarily behind a cloud, casting long shadows on the man's face. Another song began, even more popular and with a frenetic beat. He waved his arms in the air, swaying from side to side like a reed in the sea breeze.

"Boop-ya-wee-boo-ya-wee!"

I tried to push by him, but he moved to block my path, his ferret eyes even wilder.

"Wee-wee-wee!"

I stumbled backwards.

The man shambled so close, his aftershave-infused body odour made me gasp.

"Get away!"

His huge, square, block-iron head thrust forward, brow wrinkled into deep corrugations. "Boop-ya-wee-boo-ya-wee!"

His gigantic hands raised to throat level, fingers opening and closing like the pincers of a monstrous crab ready to squeeze its prey until it no longer moved.

Chapter 3

"MR CHRISTY. STOP THAT!"

A plump woman in a blue nurse's uniform hurried forward, took the man by the arm, and gently led him away. "Sorry about that, love. He gets so excited at Spring Festival, used to be a corporate accountant, but retirement changes a man."

"Thank you," I called over my shoulder at the nurse, careful not to catch the man's eye lest he broke free and came after me with those huge hands. "Must have been good for counting money: the hands, I mean."

With no job, no income, no husband, and a beach full of retirees partying like it was nineteen-ninety-nine, I felt like I'd missed the boat. If it wasn't for my landlady, Mrs Lintott, and her cat, Mr Felix, I might have quit Skegness and returned to London for a job in a corporate cubical. Here at least, the dream of a full-time reporting position flickered, although barely.

The only other highlight of an otherwise uneventful life was my Tuesday evening acting class at the Skegness Community Centre. It was run by the council, at no cost. The class officially enrolled twenty-five, but only Janet, Annabelle, and Pete showed up week in, week out.

Annabelle and Pete Brown were a retired couple. Janet was their five-year-old granddaughter. Tuesday evenings they babysat Janet, and rather than stay in their council house they brought the child to the acting class.

"I've broken into the big time," Pete announced at our last class. "Got me a role in a new production, but it is hush hush, right now. Next week I'll tell all."

I wanted to know more. Pete refused to share. Nor did Annabelle, which was unusual because she liked to talk.

"Oi!" The cry came from my right side. I glanced down to see a small boy, about seven or eight, face red, eyes narrowed in anger. He had a scar above his right eyebrow, carried an orange bucket, and waved a white spade in the air. "You stepped on my model of Tattershall Castle!"

There was a pile of muddy sand with a shallow hole. Even squinting, it was difficult to make out any structure resembling the fifteenth-century, red-brick castle in the town of Tattershall.

"Want me to help you rebuild?" I smiled.

The boy glanced at his mother, who sat reclined in a beach chair watching through dark shades. She nodded. "Tommy is into historical re-enactment and a member of the Monksthrope Little Thespian Club. He wants to build battlements, moats, bridges, and grounds for his toy knights to explore."

"That's a tall order," I said, revising my plan to dig a little hole in the sand with the child and then relax on the benches by the far wall. "How about I help get you started with one thing?"

"Sure, but you got to dig the ditch. The castle takes specialist knowledge, and my daddy is an architect, and I collect local illustrations."

For a while, digging the moat occupied my frazzled mind. It was deep and wide, and when I'd finished, I stepped back to survey it.

"Wow!" said the boy. "That's massive." He pointed towards the distant sea. "Now you gotta help me fill it with water."

"Oh no," I said, putting on my sandals. "Tommy, you are on your own on that one."

The mother laughed. "I'm Ruby Peachtree; we're from Coventry, down for a few days to visit relatives and relax. Thank you for taking the time to play with my son."

With a friendly wave and feeling good, I stepped around beach chairs, over towels and avoided more bucket and spade-wielding children.

Today I felt like the only local on a beach crowded with tourists, and that was all right with a part of me. The part that discovered a body on this beach not too long ago. That part welcomed the visitors. I shuddered at the memory and muttered a quote from Mother Teresa to keep me centred. "If you judge people, you have no time to love them." Then another from a childhood Sunday school teacher. "Love thy neighbour."

Now, with summer approaching, I hoped to put the *finding dead body thingy* behind me, get a job, and find some freelance reporting, and in that order.

Something sailed through the air, striking me on the side of the head.

"Oi, give us our Frisbee back," said a hunched man with thinning, sandy hair. He jabbed his walking stick in my direction.

"Oh, for goodness' sake," I muttered as I picked up the plastic disc and threw it at the man, hard. "Watch where you throw that damn thing."

It hit him square in the face.

"Bloody tourist!" he yelled.

I hurried away, stepping around people, eyes darting back to make sure he or other members of his elderly group weren't on my tail.

The sounds of the music, and partying from the beach grew a lot quieter as my sandals scrunched over the sand towards the benches. This part of the beach was devoid of people, just as I liked it on my regular walks.

They say in New Zealand sheep outnumber the population, same in Skegness, only it's the seagulls. A large flock of the birds, searching the sand for food, looked up occasionally.

"Peace, at last!"

I glanced at the man slumbering on the centre seat. If lady luck shone her lamp on me, he'd be a local. That would be good—we'd have a nice long moan about the tourists.

With some disappointment, I realised he was lying facedown on the wooden slats. He wore black jeans and a T-shirt with printed pineapple shapes, whose original colour might have been yellow. A dozen empty beer cans littered the ground.

"Drunk," I muttered. "The warm weather brings everyone out."

A shriek from seagulls caused me to glance up. They were circling above the bench, like a buzzard circles a fresh kill.

I shuddered despite the warm spring sunshine.

Less than twenty feet away, I called to the man. "Hello!" He seemed vaguely familiar. "Wake up, it's daytime."

Nothing.

"Sir, are you all right?"

A seagull with a crooked, yellow beak landed on the man's back. It tilted its head towards the heavens. A savage shriek sounded.

The man didn't move.

The monstrous, yellow-beaked bird hopped two steps along the man's back, stopped, and pecked at the T-shirt with a feverish vigour.

I was closer now.

Goose pimples pricked my arm.

Now a multitude of other gulls, eyes wide and eager, tiptoed towards the bench, beaks open like baby chicks at mealtime.

And then my body began to shake.

I recognised the man.

Pete Brown.

Chapter 4

A SICKLY, SOUR SENSATION bubbled in my stomach. It was a sensation I'd felt before, one which I'd hoped never to feel again. The last time my stomach roiled like this was when I found a body on the beach by the Hidden Caves Chapel.

"Pete Brown!"

He didn't move.

The seagull with the crooked, yellow beak raised its head and crowed like a victorious heavyweight boxer at the end of a championship fight. The other birds continued their advance, their feet shuffling more quickly.

My heart hammered in my chest. It was as if I was in some nightmarish dream. I pinched myself but didn't wake up.

"Please God, no!"

Somewhere I'd heard Skegness gulls delighted in devouring the eyeballs of fallen humans. I'd no idea whether that was true or how the birds could roll him over to get at his face.

None of that mattered because I would not let it happen.

I took a deep breath, fists curled into tight balls. Waving my arms, I ran forward. "Shoo, get out of here!"

The seagulls took to flight, except one—the bird with the crooked, yellow beak.

As I hurried forward, it stretched out its wings as if preparing for a fight. I swiped at it with my handbag. It let out an ear-splitting wail like a hyena denied its kill as it took to the air.

I was at the bench now.

Sweating with terror, my hand reached for my mobile phone, thankful Constable Wriggly was close by on the beach. Help would be here soon, but I doubted there was much anyone could do for Pete. I pressed the ON switch and stared at the screen saver. Mark Twain's quote flickered across the screen:

"Do the thing you fear most and the death of fear is certain."

Tears welled in my eyes as I thought of Annabelle, Pete's wife. They flowed freely as an image of his granddaughter, Janet, filled my mind. I'd tell them both I'd done everything I could. But what could I do? Then I remembered a long ago first-aid class.

I leaned forward, hand outstretched, lightly touching the man's neck to check for a pulse.

"Pete, it's Doris Cudlow."

He reared up like a mythical monster from the depths of an ancient ocean.

"Hey, that tickles!"

The words almost stopped my heart as my head went into a spin. "Pete, you're alive!"

"Of course I'm alive, Doris. What are you doing creeping up on our—"

"Jesus, Mary, and Joseph!" a voice boomed before Pete finished. "What the hell do you think you are playing out?"

A firm hand grasped my shoulder.

I spun around to see a tall, angular man with a long, narrow face. His lips were dark as if lined with a midnight-themed lipstick. A long goatee beard, raven black, tied at the end with a little pink ribbon, hung off his narrow chin. But it was his ocean-blue eyes that sent the sharpest chill along my spine. They were shining with rage like a laser beam at its target.

"Pardon," I said at a total loss for words. "I thought Pete was dead or injured or something and was about to call an ambulance and the police."

The man released his grip on my shoulder. "Lady, I don't know who the hell you think you are storming into a work of art and totally destroying it!"

Baffled, I could only echo his words. "Work of art?"

He waved his arms in a wild expression of frustration. "*Drunk Man on Bench* is to be the opening exhibit of this year's I.A. Channer exhibition."

"Please, Mr Channer, I'm sure it was a terrible mistake." The words came from a woman who'd appeared from the car park behind the benches. A plum beret covered her salt-and-pepper hair.

"Damn it all, Miss Styles. This is totally unacceptable!" Mr Channer ran a hand over his stringy, black ponytail.

The woman spoke in a soft voice as if used to soothing demanding situations. "We should be grateful there are still people in the world willing to help a person in distress."

Mr Channer turned to face me, teeth exposed like a wolf about to attack. "In a single swoop, you have ruined a day's work. Do you know how long it has taken us to get those seagulls to take an interest?"

"It is supposed to be a short silent film, shot in black and white, like one of those art house movies," chipped in Pete, now reclining on the bench, smiling. "Mr Channer, Doris is the salt of the earth. A fellow thespian, like myself."

Mr Channer threw his arms in the air. "Bloody actors! I'd have more success with dead bodies. Nobody appreciates my art, nobody!" He turned and stomped off, with the woman in the plum beret close behind.

I followed him with my eyes then turned to Pete. "What just happened?"

"The I.A. Channer experience!" Pete stood up and placed his hands on his back. "That's what I call the first encounter with our local wannabe artist celebrity."

"You're not making any sense," I said.

Pete rubbed his hands together. "I guess I'm finished for the day. Pity, Mr Channer pays thirty-five pounds an hour, and all I had to do was lie here until the seagulls took an interest. Easy money, apart from the pecking. Thank goodness Annabelle made me wear this padded T-shirt. Hot as hell, mind you. But at least the pecks didn't get through."

Now it all became clear. "Pete, is this the secret acting assignment you mentioned in class?"

"That's right. And I.A. Channer wants the wife and me as part of his opening exhibit in the Beachside Museum."

"Doing what?"

"Same as here, playing dead people."

Chapter 5

"EVERYTHING ALL RIGHT over there?" The question came from a dark-skinned woman with a huge Afro. She was standing next to a weasel-faced man with a dirty smudge of stubble smeared across his chin.

"Quite all right, thank you, just a bit of a misunderstanding, that's all," I replied. "Nothing but a little misunderstanding."

"Oh, it's just that we wondered what you were doing, intervening in the filming. I thought it was part of the script. But my friend thought otherwise." She glanced at the weasel-faced man.

"Just a simple mix-up," I repeated.

The weasel-faced man whispered in the woman's ear. She nodded. They shook hands, and hurrying, they left.

I followed them with my eyes back to the car park, where I noticed for the first time, a film camera and a small group of onlookers.

Oh bugger!

The woman in the plum beret strolled over with a broad smile on her face. "Hullo, honey, I'm Miss Jenny Styles, but everyone calls me Jenny." The sixty something-year-old woman looked like she ate suet pudding and carrot cake for breakfast, lunch, and dinner. She was short, watermelon plump, with rebellious strands of hair sticking out from beneath her beret. A pair of spectacles hung from a gold chain around her thick neck.

"Doris Cudlow," I said, extending my hand, face still warm with embarrassment. "Please call me Doris. I'm sorry about the—"

"An honest mistake, honey." Jenny took my hand and smiled. Her round face and wide hazel eyes gave her a touch of the bunny rabbit: one bubbling with vitality and a sense of humour.

"Oh, I feel such a fool." I was still blushing as I pointed towards the car park. "And it was all captured on film with a live audience!"

Jenny followed my gaze. The crowd seemed to grow by the minute.

"Oh, they've got nothing better to do. By tomorrow everyone will have forgotten all about it."

I hoped that was true and said, "I thought I'd ruined an I.A. Channer masterpiece?"

"The cameraman got the shot Mr Channer needed. To tell you the truth, we were all but done for the day; no harm done, honey."

"But Mr Channer was furious."

Jenny chuckled. "All show, sweetie. All show."

I glanced back towards the crowd to see Mr Channer with his face glistening, hands on hips, chest heaving like a rhinoceros about to attack.

"Are you sure?" I said, not yet convinced.

"Honey, the man is creative genius; they are very temperamental." Jenny adjusted her beret. "I find the starving-artist type like Mr Channer are the worst. What they lack in income they make up for in the size of their horrid attitude."

Pete, who'd remained silent, joined in the conversation. "Jenny's helping with the exhibition. More important, she handles Mr Channer and the money. Thirty-five pounds an hour, right?"

"Righto, honey. Might see if I can get you a little extra. Those seagull pecks must have hurt." Jenny's eyes crinkled in concern.

Pete rubbed his back and stooped as if in pain. "Don't like to complain, but an extra ten pounds might compensate."

Jenny said, "Poor lamb. I'll see if I can get you an additional twenty. That's the least you deserve."

Pete straightened and tilted his head in my direction as his lips tugged into a sly grin. "Network, network, network. That is the secret to acting success. How do you think I got this job?"

I said, "I'm new to town and don't have much of a network, yet."

Pete raised a finger like an English professor about to make a critical point, all concerns about his seagull-ravaged back gone. "Doris, Miss Jenny Styles is a person you need to get to know. She has connections."

Jenny laughed. "I'm just a volunteer, really, in the *Lincolnshire Weekly News* archives section at the Beachside Museum. It gives me something to do in my retirement."

Pete wagged his finger. "There is more!"

Jenny glanced back towards the car park. "Well, I teach a little, at a college in Lincoln too—French. In my free time, I visit the Skegness Hospice."

"And the exotic holidays, tell Doris about your holidays."

Jenny giggled. "Lots of vacations in the South of France."

"All right for some!" Pete grunted.

Jenny said, "Well, I'm retired and want to enjoy it."

"The farthest I can go on my pension is the beach right here in town," Pete replied. "Why else would an old bloke like me lie on a bench with empty beer cans scattered around if he wasn't short of cash?"

"I thought it was part of your plan to hit the big time in Hollywood," I said, tongue-in-cheek.

Pete snorted. "Didn't even get to taste the beer—recycled cans from the party on the beach." He jutted his chin towards Jenny. "If you can find a few more paying hard cash like Mr Channer, I might be able to vacation in France, too."

Jenny waved his comment away and turned. "Doris, the I.A. Channer exhibit opens at seven p.m. Tuesday till midnight. Would you like a free ticket?"

I enjoy live theatre shows. But museums I find a little eerie. I suppose it is all those things from long ago used by dead people.

"Oh, thank you. That is so kind." But I already knew I wouldn't go near the place, especially at night, not even if they paid me. I'd give the ticket to my landlady, Mrs Lintott. She'd relish that type of thing.

Jenny handed me a ticket along with her business card then turned to Pete. "Let's call it a day. I'll smooth things over with Mr Channer; make sure you get paid the full whack."

"Get away from me, you evil stoat!" an angry voice boomed from the car park.

We turned towards the shout.

Mr Channer waved his fists in the air like a boxer about to strike.

In front of him, with an autograph book outstretched, was a small boy.

The same boy whose castle I'd quashed and moat I'd dug.

Tommy Peachtree.

"Those bloody drawings will haunt me for life," screamed Mr Channer. "How many times do I have to tell the world that I don't do kids' stuff anymore? Now bugger off!"

The boy wiped his eyes, turned, and ran back towards the beach.

Mr Channer stooped with an abrupt movement that had in it a hint of savagery, picked up a handful of sand and threw it after the fleeing child. "Don't let me see your ugly mug again, else I'll stuff you, and put you on display in my art exhibition." Then he tipped back his head and laughed.

"If it weren't for the cash, I'd be out of here faster than a squirrel hides its nuts," Pete muttered. "But the state pension is not what it once was."

"Mr Channer is a bit of a challenge," said Jenny with a sigh. "But his art is so important to the cultural vitality of a town like Skegness. Don't you think so, Doris?"

I didn't want to verbalise my thoughts—too crude, so I said, "They say artists have tortured souls. Don't they have to suffer immensely for their art?"

Pete wrung his hands and said, "So they say. But it seems to me, Mr Channer wants others to suffer along with him."

Jenny changed the subject. "Doris, I overheard Pete mention you are a thespian?"

"Acting is a hobby. I don't have any aspirations"—I thought a little then continued—"other than playing a minor role in the occasional amateur dramatics play."

"Perfect!" Miss Styles rubbed her hands like a lawyer encouraging a client to sign. "I wonder if you'd like to be an extra in the I.A. Channer exhibit?"

"The gig pays cash," Pete offered in a hushed voice. "Away from the eyes of the taxman, if you know what I mean. They are employing actors of all ages, kids, middle aged, and old folk, like me."

Now my rational mind kicked in. I didn't have a job and needed the money. "What would I have to do?"

"Same as the wife and me," Pete said, "but in the museum at night, and there'd be no birds pecking at you there. They paid me an extra five pounds an hour for that."

"Play dead?" The words came out slow, as my mind whirred. "In a museum at night?"

"That's right," Miss Styles added. "I.A. Channer's new exhibit—*Bones in the Night, Ghosts in the Day*, comprises life-sized figurines, most skeletons, displayed in various parts of the museum. The show starts at seven and ends at midnight."

"Sounds interesting," I said as I considered the many bills I could tackle with the cash.

Jenny lowered her voice. "The engineers are installing the exhibits as we speak, and we have our first run-through with the actors this evening. Would you care to join us?" Before I answered, she added, "And I'd see to it you get a little extra for your inconvenience today. Are you in?"

I thought about the money, thought about my bills, then I thought of I.A. Channer's treatment of Tommy Peachtree, and my stomach roiled.

"No, thank you."

Chapter 6

IT WASN'T UNTIL I PARKED my Nissan Micra in the street outside Whispering Towers Boarding House that my heartbeat returned to normal and my stomach settled. I couldn't stand the mistreatment of children.

Neither did I want to be at the centre of rumours about a madwoman storming an art exhibit. Especially since Skegness is a small town; I needed a job, and rumours spread like wildfire.

As I climbed out of the car, I thought about a long hot relaxing shower.

"The best way to put the events of the morning behind me."

Mr Felix, the landlady's cat, sat in his usual spot at the top of the steps by the entrance. He rubbed against my leg as I reached for the door key.

"All good in your cat kingdom?"

The cat purred.

I felt a little better.

Once I'd showered and taken a nap, all would be good in my world too. Then suitably rested I'd spend the rest of the day on my computer. The search for a job was the top priority. It wasn't exactly a jam-packed agenda, but it was all I had, given my limited financial circumstances.

I opened the door, stepping into the dark hallway. The scent of dampness, mould, and leftover cooking filled my nostrils. A homely smell, I thought, letting out a breath I didn't realise I was holding.

On tiptoe, I hurried along the hallway. I didn't want to speak to anyone, not least the landlady, whose door I'd just passed. Mrs Lintott likes to play matchmaker in my life, and that was another thing I could do without right now.

My bedsit apartment was up a narrow staircase. I eased my foot on the first step then slowly shuffled onto the second.

It creaked.

"Yoo hoo, Doris, is that you?" Mrs Lintott hurried out into the hall. "I thought I heard you on the stairs."

I made a helpless gesture with my hands and turned around. "Good afternoon, Mrs Lintott. Another fine day outside."

Mrs Lintott folded her arms. "Been for your regular stroll along the seafront?"

"Yes, unusually crowded for this time of year," I replied.

"The Retirees' Spring Festival, best avoid it, love. Did you have a good time?"

"So-so. You know how it gets with all those crowds."

Mrs Lintott tugged at her ear. "One of my bingo ladies called to say she saw you dancing barefoot on the beach with an older gentleman."

"Everyone was dancing. It was a bit of fun." That wasn't exactly the truth, but I didn't want to explain.

"Doris, I know your love life is a bit of a disaster, but isn't Mr Christy a touch old for you?" There was a tinge of disappointment in Mrs Lintott's voice.

"Mr Christy?"

"The man you were dancing barefoot with. He's a retired accountant, love. Took up taxidermy when he retired. Nasty preservative smell about him, like a mortuary, and stuffing dead things... well, at your age, you need a bit more excitement than that. Why don't you let me fix you up with one of our town's single businessmen? How about the funeral director, Mr—"

"No!" I barked.

Mrs Lintott scratched her head in a bemused fashion. "Doris, you can't trust a man with large hands."

I frowned. "Why can't I walk the beach, meet a man with large hands, and dance barefoot without one of your spies reporting my activity?"

"Bad morning, eh? Come inside, and we can talk all about it. There's nothing like a nice cuppa to help lift your mood."

"Sorry, Mrs Lintott, but I've got a lot on today."

"Like what?"

That stumped me. "A shower... err... a nap... err... then I begin my job search." It sounded pathetic. It was.

Mrs Lintott sniffed. "Mrs McLaughlin called. She's one of my bingo ladies. Her husband, Jack, is in the Skegness Model Railway Club with Pete Brown. You know Pete, don't you?"

"Yes, he is in my acting class." My mind whirred as I tried to figure out where Mrs Lintott was going with this. "I didn't know he knew Mr McLaughlin."

"It's a small town, love. Even if you try to hide, someone will spot you in the end." In an unconscious gesture Mrs Lintott moistened her lips. "Mrs McLaughlin says you turned down an acting job for the I.A. Channer exhibition. That's not true, is it?"

"Well... err... yes."

"But you need a job, love." Mrs Lintott stood there, arms folded, waiting.

I told her what I'd seen and how Mr Channer treated the little boy, Tommy. I left out any mention of seagulls or ruining a work of art.

Mrs Lintott listened in silence.

"Mr Channer may well be a renowned artist," I said to conclude, "but I find his manner repulsive. I can't work for a man who abuses children like that."

Mrs Lintott pursed her lips. "Come on, Doris, we'd better have a cuppa in my kitchen. I've got something important to tell you."

Chapter 7

MRS LINTOTT FILLED a kettle with water, putting it on the stove. While the water heated, she busied herself preparing a tray. After a short while, the kettle whistled, and she filled a large teapot. Then she picked up the tray and carried it to the kitchen table, lowering herself down into a chair.

As she poured out two cups of tea into china mugs, she said, "Doris, I've come across some repulsive characters in my life. One thing I've learned is that it does no good to run or hide; best lance the boil, and be done with it."

I hadn't thought about my reaction to Mr Channer's treatment of Tommy Peachtree as running—maybe that's just what I did, what I've always done. I left my marriage, left London, and now I'd let the opportunity of a little paid employment slip between my fingers rather than confront a loutish man. Maybe running away from difficult circumstances was part of my makeup. That was an uncomfortable thought, one I didn't like.

I said, "What would you have done?"

Mrs Lintott tutted then picked up her cup. "Never trust a man with ribbons in his beard. Nor a former magician. Mr Channer used to perform in a magic show."

"Like Harry Houdini?"

"That's right, love. He had his own show."

I thought about Mr Channer's long, narrow face and goatee beard tied with ribbons. "He surely has the flair for it, almost like an old-fashioned showman. Yes, I can see him on stage in his own magic showcase."

Mrs Lintott nodded. "Over the years I've seen 'em magic away hundreds of people. Once I saw a man riding a motorbike vanish. That was a David Copperfield show. Never been able to figure it out. Those magicians like to keep their illusions a secret."

I blew on the surface of the mug. "What tricks did Mr Channer do in his show?"

Mrs Lintott's lips tugged up at the edges, ready to share a nugget of gossip. "It was a tiny affair, amateur really, with lots of cloaks and things vanishing. It was supposed to be for children, but it wasn't suitable."

"Why not?"

"Too many complaints from the parents."

I gave Mrs Lintott a long curious look. "What types of complaints?"

"I'm not one to spread gossip, so I'll say no more than Mr Channer doesn't get along with children."

I thought back to Mr Channer's treatment of Tommy Peachtree and had to know more. "What didn't the parents like about the show?"

Mrs Lintott moistened her lips. "Most children magicians make a rabbit disappear in a black top hat. Then it reappears somewhere else."

"Oh yes, I've seen that."

"Mr Channer did the same thing... with a chicken."

"A rubber chicken?"

"No, a live hen. He placed it in the hat, waved a magic wand, and the bird disappeared."

"What's the trouble with that?"

"He wrung its neck before placing it in the magic hat."

"My God!"

Mrs Lintott's eyes glittered with the satisfaction of a nugget of gossip perfectly delivered, but I knew by the curl of her lips there was more. "Oooh, Doris, it was terrible. I can scarcely bring myself to say it."

"Say what?"

"When Mr Channer waved his magic wand a second time, the bird reappeared... as a bucket of fried chicken!"

We fell into silence for several minutes.

At last Mrs Lintott blew on the surface of her tea, took a sip and shrugged. "We don't have to like the people we work with. If that was a requirement we'd still be living in caves. Why don't you contact Miss Jenny Styles and tell her you've changed your mind. If Mr Channer gets up to his nasty tricks with you or anyone else, call the bugger out."

That was logical. Given my jobless circumstance, it all made sense. I stirred some sugar into my tea. "I suppose you're right."

Mrs Lintott's eyes met mine. "Do you have her number?"

"Jenny gave me her business card; it's in my handbag. I'll call her after my shower."

"Call her now!"

Mrs Lintott uttered those three little words with such authority I reached for my handbag, pulled out the business card, and dialled.

"Hello, Miss Styles, this is Doris Cudlow... Very well, thank you... Yes... Yes... About the acting job... Uh-huh... Uh-huh... I see... Okay, I understand... Enjoy the exhibition."

I hung up and shook my head. "Nothing doing. The acting slots are all taken. They begin their rehearsal this evening at ten."

Mrs Lintott refilled her cup. "Guess we must go to plan B."

"Plan B?"

"Doris, you can't survive long in Skegness without money or a job. There is the rent to pay, food to buy, petrol for your car, and your daily beach walks are not enough. You need to join a gym."

Exercise wasn't my favourite activity. The thought of pounding the treadmill or stationary bike under artificial light sent a shudder down my spine. "Not my thing. Why would I waste money on a gym?"

Mrs Lintott didn't answer immediately but sat there stirring sugar into her tea. "Doris, I don't like to mention this, but you've gained rather a few pounds since moving to Skegness—all those doughnuts from your overnight shift at Fantasy Gardens Arcade, no doubt."

"Mrs Lintott, I challenge anyone to lose weight while cooking doughnuts for a living. It's impossible!" I turned to look out of the kitchen window. "Anyway, that job's on hold since the town closed down the place. I might be a little late with the rent because—"

She raised a hand. "That's why you need to snatch every job opportunity that comes your way. You'll need every penny to pay for a gym membership and a personal trainer. You are too young to let yourself go to the dogs."

"I can hardly afford the rent, let alone gym membership," I said, ignoring her comment about going to the dogs.

Mrs Lintott finished her tea and put down the cup with great care. "That is why I have put fifty pounds down on your behalf."

"My behalf?"

"Do you know Mrs Addison, from Jamaica—large Afro? She saw you destroy the I.A. Channer art exhibit on the beach this morning. What were you thinking?"

I kept my mouth firmly shut. If the incident had reached Mrs Lintott's ear, then it wouldn't be long before it was all over town.

Mrs Lintott waited, looking at me with a tiny knowing smile on her face. After a long moment, she said, "The postie has opened a book. I've had a little flutter."

The postman, Gary, known by all as the postie, is a weasel-faced man with a dirty smudge of stubble smeared across his chin, a twitching nose, and garlic breath. He delivers the mail early and spends the rest of the day in Bet Quick Bookies on Ida Road.

"Oh no!" My voice rose in panic. "What type of bet?"

Mrs Lintott's smile broke out into a full-out grin. "A little flutter we can easily win!" She lowered her voice. "I've put fifty quid down that you won't destroy any more of Mr Channer's art exhibits before next week's bank holiday weekend. I've called around my bingo ladies. They couldn't slap their cash down fast enough."

"Mrs Lintott, no!"

She drained her cup then let out a wild laugh. "Doris, this week we're going to take the postie to the cleaners!"

Chapter 8

I TOOK A LONG HOT SHOWER to begin to wash away the memories of the day. After a nap, I pulled open my laptop, slouched on my sofa bed, and searched for jobs. It must have been an hour later that my mobile phone rang.

I turned away from the laptop, walked to the kitchen table and picked up the phone.

"Hello?"

"Doris, is that you? This is Grace Rivers."

Grace worked as a security guard at the Beachside Museum. We'd become friends after a close call with a murderous killer.

"What's up, Grace?"

There was a long pause. "Doris, I've got a big favour to ask."

"For you, anything." And I meant it. It is not every day the person who saved your life asks for a favour. "You name it, and I'll do my best."

"It's Joey, my son..."

"What happened?"

Grace's voice trembled. "Doctor Bellamy came to visit. Joey has a temperature."

"Will he be all right?"

"Yes, he will be fine, just a virus. There is nothing we can do except make him comfortable."

I made a sympathetic noise then said, "So sorry, poor Joey. Is there anything I can do?"

"I have to work tonight but can't leave Joey, I wonder if you—"

"Of course," I said interrupting. "I'd be delighted to look after your son. What time do you want me to show up?"

Grace let out an anxious chuckle. "Doris, that is so sweet, but that's not why I called."

"Oh, go on," I said, pressing the phone to my ear. "You know I'll do anything to help you."

She spoke slowly, as if not wanting to continue. "I called to ask if you could take my overnight shift at the Beachside Museum?"

"Oh!" There was no way I was spending the night locked inside a spooky museum. "Work your overnight shift at Beachside?"

"Just until Joey is a little better."

"I thought you worked the day shift?"

"I did, but the boss moved me to nights, starting today."

"Why?" The question popped out of my mouth before I could restrain it.

There was a long silence. "Cheryl Moore quit. She was the weekend overnight security guard in the archives section. The boss wants me to fill in, but I can't, at least not tonight."

"I see," I said but sensed there was something she wasn't telling me. "How are you?"

"Stressed, you know how that goes." Grace let out another chuckle; it sounded tired and nervous. "Are there any vacancies on your doughnut shift at Fantasy Gardens Arcade?"

"Sorry, the place closed down. At least for now. The owner, Mr Hornsby, is in all sorts of regulatory trouble."

"Shame, I really need another job."

"Me too, girl."

"So you'll take my shift?"

I cleared my throat. "Wouldn't you rather have me look after Joey? I have a first-aid certificate?"

Grace didn't say anything at first. Then she said, "Joey needs his mother."

I couldn't argue with that and said, "But Grace, I'm not trained as a security guard."

"All you have to do is sit at the desk outside the *Lincolnshire Weekly News* archives section and walk around every fifteen minutes to check on things, nothing more."

"What if something happens?"

Another long silence. "Nothing ever happens."

"Oh Grace, I'm so sorry... I just can't." But there was more to it than that. My hesitation was also in part because of Fred Faul.

I met Fred at the *Skegness Telegraph*.

We clashed on my first day.

Fred thought the newspaper was about to make him an offer as a reporter when I showed up. But he'd only ever written one story, and that was when he was seven or eight. Middle aged, he'd worked as a security guard all his adult life. Frankly, I found him a little creepy—the *get under your skin and annoy the hell out of you* kind of creepy.

Fred moonlighted as a security guard at the Beachside Museum.

"Doris, I've nowhere else to turn. If I don't find a replacement for tonight I'll be fired. I'm drowning in credit card debt. I need this job." Grace's ragged voice was almost a whimper. "Please don't run away from me."

That did it.

I would not let Grace down because I might bump into Fred Faul—not now, not ever. Pushing thoughts of a night in a darkened, eerie museum to the back of my mind, I took a deep breath and put on my best New York accent. "Yes, girlfriend, I can do that. I've got your back for as long as you need me to stand in for you."

"Doris, you are wonderful. Without this job, me and Joey would be out on the street." Her voice broke, and she sobbed for a moment. "I really need another job, ideally in the day."

I said, "Can't be easy, bringing up a child on your own."

"I've made my own bed, doing the best I can with it." Grace cleared her throat. "I've spoken with the boss, and he is fine, so long as you do as he says."

"I must be mad!"

Grace laughed. "To tell you the truth, the work is boring. If I didn't need the money, I'd never do it."

"Dull work beats unemployed in my book. Give me the details."

"The shift starts at ten p.m. tonight. Get there a little early and report to Captain Honeybush."

"Captain who?"

"Honeybush. He served in the army, won lots of medals. He is the boss. Like I say, get there early as Mr Channer and the actors have a dry run through their art exhibition."

I closed my eyes and shuddered at the memory of the odious artist. Nothing was worse in my book than the mistreatment of children. Had the man forgotten he was once a boy? "Anything else I should know?"

Grace didn't answer for a long while, and when she did it was in a hushed whisper. "Try not to be alone with Captain Honeybush. He's creepy."

Chapter 9

THE BEACHSIDE MUSEUM was a Victorian building. Half lighthouse, half country mansion it was run by the Skegness Trust for Historic Buildings. The car park was pitch black as I pulled my Nissan Micra into a parking space near the front entrance. It was nine forty-five at night, and I wanted to be as close to the front door as possible.

"Lots of dark places where people can jump out at you," I muttered, staring out of the windscreen. "They need security guards for the security guards!"

For a moment I stared into the mirror and adjusted my hair. Tonight, I felt underdressed in blue jeans and a cream blouse.

"Just wear a nice plain blouse and comfortable flat shoes," Grace had said. "The museum will give you a uniform."

A warm wind blew in from the sea as I hurried towards the entrance where a dull light illuminated the front door. I glanced back to make sure there was no one in the shadows. Then I tilted my head to the heavens. A cloudless sky filled with millions of dots twinkled back.

After several moments of wonder, I glanced at the entrance door, reached out for the handle and pushed.

It didn't move.

I pushed again.

"Definitely locked."

There was no doorbell, so I leaned on the plate-glass window to peer inside. The main lobby was dimly lit. To one side was a small gift shop and in the centre, a large counter with a huge overhead sign:

INFORMATION SERVICE
Beachside Museum is delighted to help you.
Museum hours 9am-8pm daily.
Closed Sunday
Customer service is our only priority!
COMING THIS TUESDAY: I.A. Channer exhibition—*Bones in the Night, Ghosts in the Day (7pm to Midnight)*

Underneath the sign, seated at the desk, sat a uniformed man. His head rested on his arms as if in deep thought. I stepped back, going over in my mind Grace River's instructions. "Take the front steps; the actors will probably already be there, but I'll have the guard on duty leave the door open for you."

I banged on the window, hard.

The figure's head shot up. With movements like a slow-motion sports replay, he stood up, glanced around as if dazed, then sat back down.

I knocked again and shouted.

The security guard glanced in my direction. With sluggish movements he lumbered towards the door. As he drew close, I noticed his crumpled uniform, scuffed shoes, and uncombed hair. Then I let out an annoyed breath. "Fred Faul!"

At the door, Fred peered through the glass, his nervous eyes darting from me to the space behind as if he thought there might be others hiding in the dark.

He opened the door a crack, the air filled with the whiff of cheap alcohol. Fred bawled, "What the hell do you want?"

"Polite as always, Fred. Now let me in."

"The museum is closed." He pointed to the sign that hung above the reception desk. "I'd have thought a journalist like you would have been able to read. But then again, I thought I'd get the job as a newspaper reporter for the *Skegness Telegraph*."

"Fred, the newspaper closed down," I said in a calm, slow voice. "Can we let bygones be bygones?"

Fred thought for a moment, furrowing his brow. "I'll never forget what happened. It is seared deep into my memory. My one chance at Easy Street and you snatched it right out of my grasp."

"But you worked on the reception desk as the security guard, not a reporter."

Fred's eyes glazed over as if drawing on a distant memory. "Don't suppose you know my elementary school story about speaking fruit came top of the class?"

"Are you going to let me in?"

"'Revenge of the Fruit Bowl'; that's what I called it, got a commendation from the headmaster for my characterisation of Mr Plum and Mrs Apple."

Now wasn't the time to discuss the merits of Fred's childhood story about fruit wreaking vengeful havoc on mankind. "Fred, I'm standing in for Grace Rivers tonight."

Silence.

When the silence continued to stretch, I cleared my throat and repeated the sentence. "Tonight, I'm standing in for Grace Rivers. Captain Honeybush is expecting me."

Fred's eyes cleared. He folded his arms, and barely able to hide his shock said, "You! Well, I never! Isn't it enough you stole my one chance at reporting success right from under my nose. Now you want to take a bite out of my security job too!"

I tried to smooth things over. "Fred, it is only temporary. Just for tonight, while Grace cares for her son, Joey."

Fred's face grew red. "This takes the biscuit. Don't you know I'm an artist? I should be reclining on a oceanside veranda with a glass of sangria in my hand. How will I ever reach my potential if people like you keep holding me back?"

I swallowed the lump of annoyance growing in my throat. "There is no way I'll step on your toes or get in your way. We can work together as security personnel." Then I added, with fingers crossed, "It will be fun."

It didn't work.

Fred's eyes filled with the irrational rage of a rush-hour motorist. "Nothing is safe from your rampaging paws!"

I stepped forward. "Fred, let me in."

But he slammed the door.

It clicked shut with a sharp *thwack*.

I watched with irritation as Fred stomped back into the lobby.

"That didn't go well," I muttered as he disappeared around a corner.

The question was what to do about it.

Chapter 10

AS I WAS PONDERING my options, Fred returned. At his side, striding like a drill sergeant, was a tall walrus of a man in his late fifties, although he might have been older. With a chubby face and a thin, waxed moustache over his plump lips, the man looked like an overfed Victorian portrait. He carried a polished cane in one hand, and his dark blue uniform with golden tassels was immaculate—sharp crease in the trousers, with the silver metal buttons on his jacket so shiny he must have just polished them.

The chubby man signalled to Fred, who opened the door.

"Mrs Cudlow, I take it?" He spoke with an Oxbridge accent, all nasal and superior. "The name's Captain Napoleon Honeybush." He peered down his bulbous turned-up nose. "Served in the Lancashire Fusiliers."

I felt as if I should curtsy or bow or something but said, "Grace Rivers mentioned you were okay with me standing in." I glanced at Fred. "Temporarily."

Fred snorted but said nothing else.

The captain stared at me with beady, brown eyes. They were like two peanuts set in a mound of risen bread dough. "Have you ever worked as a security guard in a museum?"

"No." I'd come across the Captain Honeybush type before. They are happiest with short answers, don't like questions.

Captain Honeybush laced his fat fingers and looked down frowning. "Can you follow simple instructions?"

The man's uppity tone was already annoying, but I said, "Yes."

He paused and placed a thick finger at the side of his mouth. "I run a disciplined ship; no time for slackers. Rule number one, the captain gives the orders, and you follow. Is that clear, Old Gal?"

"Right you are." Now wasn't the time to get fussy over being called an old gal. "I'll do the best job possible, sir."

He smoothed down the corners of his waxy moustache with a thumb and forefinger. "Very good, Old Gal. Fred, you get back to your duties. Mrs Cudlow, you follow me. We've got to find you a uniform. We keep them in the storeroom. A little dark in there, but we'll manage."

Fred returned to the front desk, face red, and muttering.

"This way, Old Gal." The captain pointed with his cane at a distant staircase.

Alarm bells rang as I remembered Grace's caution not to be alone with the man. But he walked with a limp I could outrun, so I followed him at a distance.

The captain's polished shoes cheeped as he strode, and his cane struck the concrete floor with a rhythmic clap.

Tap-tap-tap.

At the top of the stairs, that led to the second floor, he paused, half turned. "It is Mrs Cudlow, isn't it?" His eyes settled on my empty ring finger.

None of your bloody business, I thought, but said, "My ex-husband works in London."

A shine came to his eye, and his thick lips slowly formed into a smile. "A spurned woman? Well, not to worry, Old Gal. Lots of fillies must work these days, you know. Do an excellent job for old Honeybush, and I'll see you all right."

"I'll do my best," I said, growing uncomfortable at the gleam in his tiny peanut eyes.

"Very good. Now, let's get started." As the captain stared at my face, his smile swelled into a grin. With a practised movement he reached out a plump hand and patted my butt. "Things are going swimmingly so far, don't you think? Why don't you leave me your address, and phone number."

I was about to tell the pompous creep where he could stuff the job when a voice called out.

"Hullo, Doris!"

Jenny Styles hurried up the stairs. Out of breath the short, plump woman said, "Grace mentioned you'd be stepping in for her." She adjusted the plum beret. "So sorry to hear about little Joey; he must feel awful. It's not nice when you're sick."

The captain coughed. "I was just taking Mrs Cudlow into the storeroom... to choose a uniform."

Jenny's eyes grew hard and cold as she tugged her glasses from her face. "Captain, I'm sure a man with your responsibilities has more pressing work to do in your office. I'll show Mrs Cudlow to the uniform area and help her pick out suitable attire."

There was an awkward silence.

"Very well." Captain Honeybush frowned, turned, and walked back towards the lobby, his cane rapping against the hard concrete floor like an angry woodpecker.

At the steps, the captain stopped and said, "Miss Styles, please show Mrs Cudlow her other duties. Only the main archives area, no need to patrol the storerooms. Is that understood?"

"As you wish, honey," Jenny replied, giving a mock salute.

Captain Honeybush pointed his cane and growled, "I'll check in on you both when I do my midnight rounds."

Then he turned and walked away.

Tap-tap-tap.

As the sound echoed off into the distance, I let out a long sigh. If it weren't for Grace and Joey, I'd have quit right there and then. But my friend needed my help. I wasn't about to run away.

Whatever happened tonight I'd see it through.

I had a plan.

It was simple.

Stay as far away from Captain Honeybush as humanly possible.

My only worry was he had the opposite intention.

Chapter 11

WE WERE DEEP INSIDE the storeroom. It was dark and smelled of dust, mould, and plastic. Cabinets, broken chairs, wooden tables, and old computers littered the space. Boxes, crates, and tins crammed every shelf.

"My God, the captain's creepy," I said as we navigated the gloom with the aid of a low-wattage light bulb.

"Men like Captain Honeybush should have died out with the street gas lamp," Jenny replied. "Sadly, there are still a few around in the darkened corners of certain old-world country clubs. They cling on to the old boys' network and use it mercilessly for position and privilege. The captain is good friends with Judge Eboch! You can't get better connected around these parts than that."

We stopped at a row of metal shelves. Jackets covered in plastic wrapping hung from a rail.

Jenny said, "Captain Honeybush got the job as head of museum security on account of his army service; you know how that goes."

"That's a relief," I said in a mocking tone. "Because if the captain is the best man for the job, I'm a Skegness seagull!"

Jenny giggled. "Don't speak too soon, honey. The captain is so well connected he can get away with anything. Tonight you might just sprout feathers and start squawking."

We both laughed. But there was something in her words that sent a little chill along my spine.

Jenny straightened, placed her hands on her hips, and said, "Honey, that man could commit murder and walk away scot-free. He is what they call in French un gentleman intouchable—an untouchable gentleman. Do you know how many security guards have left on account of his creepiness?"

"No one is outside of the law," I said, wondering how Grace put up with working in this place.

Jenny tugged the chain of her spectacles. "Not a lot of light in here, I'm afraid. Pick out a jacket and trousers from the rack. The belts, caps, and ties are in the boxes, all brand new."

I scanned the boxes for my hat size. "Why so many uniforms?"

"The captain ordered them years ago. He claimed they were a steal. The truth is he bought from an old army friend. Old boys' network once again."

I'd had enough of Captain Honeybush, so I changed the subject. "What keeps you here?"

"Oh, me? I'm retired. Volunteering gives me something to do. One day I'd like to run a class on the history of local art right here in the museum. Oh, and I like to keep a close eye on the captain."

It was clear Jenny wasn't ready to change the subject, so I said, "Why don't people complain?"

"They do. The problem is nothing sticks to the man. He is like Teflon."

I said, "Old boys' network?"

Jenny nodded. "That's why I took the position as the museum's official archivist, to keep an eye on the man. It's been ten years, though, and he's been getting away with all sorts."

"Where am I patrolling this evening?" I asked, again trying to change the subject.

"The *Lincolnshire Weekly* archives section. Have you used it?"

"Oh yes," I said, thankful we'd moved on from the captain. But the words came out a little too enthusiastic, so I added, "The archives were a little difficult to navigate, but I found what I needed."

Jenny frowned. "The museum set up the cataloguing system years ago. I've added to it and made rather a muddle of things, I'm afraid. If you're interested, I run a class on using the archives, with the local school."

"Thank you, but if I need anything from the archives, I know who to call."

Jenny chuckled. "You saw right through my recruitment pitch, eh? The archives are a sacred space to local historians. They store knowledge about our area that is all too easily lost." She paused to look me in the eye. "I'm also a volunteer at the Skegness Hospice. We are short of volunteers; can I interest you?"

"That takes a special person. I'm not sure I'd bring much cheer."

Jenny let out a disappointed murmur and pointed towards the clothes. "Why don't you look and take out the items you want."

I picked out a jacket, trousers, and a new cream blouse along with a cap and dark blue, clip-on tie. "This should do the job."

"There is a changing room at the back. I'll wait for you here."

The changing room was a small area filled with yet more boxes and metal shelves. A curtain pole with a thin sheet served as a privacy shield. As I slipped out of my jeans, I heard a loud creak, followed by a quiet thud.

I said into the darkness, "Do you think the museum will run your history of local art class?"

"Funding is too tight," Jenny replied. After a moment, she added, "I suppose things might change if we get more visitors, but even Old Betty doesn't generate much interest these days."

Chapter 12

"WHO IS OLD BETTY?" I was back in the central area with Jenny.

"The ghost of the housekeeper of the first owner, a property developer from London, can't recall his name. They say she always carried a broom in her large, calloused hands and was like a machine for keeping the place in order." Jenny spoke fast, her voice brimming with enthusiasm.

I glanced around the clutter of the storeroom. "Seems like we could do with Old Betty's abilities in here. What happened to her?"

"When the property developer sold the place, she stayed on keeping house for the new owners. They were from Bordeaux in France. The family lived here for twenty years. When they left for America, the county council bought the property. Betty was getting on in age by then, but the council kept her on."

Not that I'm one of those people who believe in ghosts, but there was something unique about Old Betty. I said, "She sounds like an interesting woman. I wonder if anyone has written her life story?"

Jenny thought for a moment, furrowing her brow. "Not that I know of... but it would make a fascinating article for our local history section." She reached out a hand to a nearby box and ran her finger over the top. Staring at the dust, she said, "I'm sure it would interest the *Lincolnshire Weekly News*. Once in a while, they run a local history column."

Curious, I said, "Do you have any photographs?"

Jenny touched her cheek. "Yes, somewhere in the archives. Once we're settled in for the night, I'll dig them out."

"That would be wonderful," I said as the idea of writing the article myself took shape in my mind.

"Righto, honey. That'll give us something to chat about."

I said, "Don't suppose you know the editor of the *Lincolnshire Weekly News* by any chance?"

"That'd be Marcus Baker. He is such a fun person to be around, knows everything about Skegness history. I guess he must be in his late seventies by now."

"A fountain of knowledge, then?" All at once my spirits lifted, confident Marcus Baker would buy my article. Who knows, I thought with growing excitement, it might even lead to a full-time position.

"Honey, he's so old. I think he might even have met Old Betty."

"Oh, I'd love to meet Marcus, pitch an article to him about Old Betty." I smiled invitingly.

"Righto honey, I'll mention it to him for you."

"Only if it is not too much trouble," I said, trying to hide my excitement. I made a mental note to begin work on the article when I woke up in the morning. This felt like I was on to something special. "Old Betty sounds like a real character."

"Yep, and she worked here at the Beachside Museum until a few days before her death."

"How old was she when she passed?"

"One hundred and seven."

"My goodness!" I said, unable to conceal my astonishment. "They don't make 'em like that anymore."

The laugh that came from Jenny sounded hollow, almost eerie. "They say Old Betty's ghost walks the museum to this day."

I'd heard ghosts stalk places where tragedy struck, so I said, "Why would she haunt the museum?"

Jenny shrugged and put on her reading glasses. "Checking to see things are in order, I suppose."

I gazed around at the cluttered space. If Old Betty's ghost existed, it would haunt this storeroom. That thought caused another, one I couldn't help but ask.

"Jenny, have you heard of the Dancing Hands Mystery?"

"Oh, yes, honey," she said, spacing out her words as if in deep thought. "Must have been ten years ago when Fiona Fenchurch was"—her voice dropped an octave—"killed, right here on the Skegness beach."

"What happened?"

Jenny peered at me through her reading glasses and snorted. "The policeman who saw the whole thing reckons Old Betty dragged Fiona's body into the sea."

"That's bizarre," I said, trying to sound astonished. And I would have been if it were not for Constable Wriggly's account on the beach earlier. "What do you think happened?"

Jenny didn't answer immediately but twiddled with her reading glasses as if she was considering whether to share what was on her mind.

"Police cover-up."

The words came out like a breath of air, barely audible. My first thought was that I'd misheard. "Pardon?"

Jenny cast a glance over her shoulder. In a hurried whisper, she said, "The old boys 'network. The killer was a member of the insider's club. Strings were pulled, and Judge Eboch let the killer walk away scot-free."

I wondered whether her utterings were the product of an over imaginative mind, so I said, "What makes you say that?"

Jenny tapped the side of her nose. Words tumbled out of her mouth like an erupting volcano. "Honey, a murder took place on a crowded beach; the body disappeared in broad daylight, and the officer in charge reckons a ghost dragged it into the sea! Whoever was behind the Dancing Hands Mystery was either a magician or had lots of political connections."

"I don't buy into magic," I said.

"Me neither." Jenny adjusted her reading glasses. "So, it stands to reason the murderer was a member of the old boys' network."

Chapter 13

A LOT HAD HAPPENED since my morning stroll on the beach through the crowds of the Retirees' Spring Festival. If it weren't for my feet, which still ached, I'd have thought I was in some bizarre dream. But this was no dream. I was in a dimly lit storeroom, in the bowels of a museum dressed in a security guard's uniform, ready for my overnight stay.

The light in the storeroom dimmed as I said, "Jenny, have you seen the ghost of Old Betty?"

"Let's not talk about that, honey. It was a long time ago."

"So you saw something, then?" I said as the light flickered brighter.

Jenny turned away. "Only an icy chill."

"Like the breeze from an air-conditioning unit?"

Jenny shook her head. "More like a frozen metal bar running down my spine. Followed by the sound of something."

A lump came to my throat. "What type of sound?"

"It was nothing, really." The tremble in Jenny's voice didn't sound like nothing.

"Nothing?"

Jenny gave me a look, enigmatic, half smiling. "Honey, it was nothing at all."

"But you heard a noise?"

She puffed out her cheeks. "Oh, Doris, let's not be silly and start scaring each other. It was nothing."

I shivered then said, "This sound, was it like a... voice wailing into the night?"

"Nope. Not a voice." Jenny shrugged her shoulders with a gesture of resignation. "A kind of clanking noise like a... chain rattling."

"Where did you hear it?"

"In the *Lincolnshire Weekly News* archives section."

I made a slow-blowing sound through my lips. "Did you see anything?"

Jenny reached out an arm and leaned against a shelf. "It only happened once, about ten years ago."

I took a moment to consider that. Then I said, "What did you see?"

Jenny's breathing became heavy as if a weight pressed hard against her chest. When she spoke, it was without her usual bubble, and her round face was ghastly pale.

"I saw something wispy, like a white mist. Maybe it was nothing more than a cloud of dust." But her pale face and trembling voice told me otherwise.

My heart beat faster. "Oh my goodness. Was it in the form of a woman... Old Betty?"

"It could have been anything. I'm sure it was nothing at all. You know how the mind likes to play tricks?"

Something clinked near the door.

"Stop right there!" Jenny yelled.

"Oh, I'm so sorry, Old Gal. I... err... forgot... err... you and Mrs Cudlow were in here."

Tap-tap-tap.

When we could no longer hear the captain's cane, Jenny said, "Doris, are you okay?"

I wanted to say, everything is tickety boo, but the hairs on the back of my neck stood up, and my stomach roiled. "The captain creeps me out more than the thought of seeing Old Betty."

Jenny let out a long sigh. "Me too, but don't worry about him. Stick with me, and we'll both be fine."

Her words, meant to be soothing, riled up my nerves to a higher level. "Won't the captain come creeping about later, to check on us?"

Jenny's lips tugged upward into a mutinous curve. "The man's a creature of habit and as lazy as a hog in the sunshine. He'll be in his office knocking back a brandy or three. After his evening tipple, he'll nap until the morning. You won't see him again tonight."

I wasn't so sure. "How do you know Captain Honeybush won't wake up and come sneaking about the place... drunk?"

Jenny tapped her nose. "Trust me, once he's had his favourite tipple, he'll be out for the count. Happens every time the captain works the overnight shift."

If I hadn't been paying attention, I would have missed it, that slight rise in tone, almost imperceptible twitch at the corner of her lips. "Jenny, are you saying you put something in the captain's drink?"

A gleam of dancing mischief filled her eyes. "Wouldn't want him creeping about after dark annoying the ladies, now, would we, honey?"

Chapter 14

MY GUT WAS TELLING me that Jenny's doctoring of the captain's night-time tipple wouldn't be enough to ensure an uneventful night. It'd been ten years since Old Betty's last haunting of the archives; maybe she was due a return. The thought kept me on edge as we made our way through the museum towards the *Lincolnshire Weekly News* archives area.

We hurried by gigantic cases, paintings hung in ornate frames, and multimedia cinema-style rooms relaying highlights of Skegness history. Jenny walked fast, nimble for her age. My feet still hurt from earlier on the beach, so I lagged a few steps behind.

After another set of stairs, we turned into a large room filled with bodies—hundreds of them. Some were fully fleshed, others little more than bones.

"What on earth!" I said, walking by a skeleton in a dark blue, pinstriped business suit, a briefcase in one hand and black bowler hat in the other.

"I.A. Channer's model figures," Jenny replied with a smooth wave of the hand. "These are waiting to be installed. The work crew will set them up before we open to the public on Tuesday."

We stood there staring at the models. They were mostly adults dressed in everyday clothes. I spotted a tennis player, a taxi driver, and a schoolteacher. There was even a coal miner. I scanned the room in search of a newspaper reporter—nothing—but I spotted a stooped figure in dark clothes carrying a large pole—a Victorian gas lamplighter. And there were a few children, most school aged. One child caught my eye. He reminded me of someone, but I couldn't think who.

"Look at this!" Jenny said, pointing at a businessman mannequin.

"Very realistic," I said, peering into its face. "If I didn't know any better, I'd be on the phone to the police. He looks like a real business person."

"Didn't fool me in the slightest, honey."

"Are you serious?" I said as I continued to glance around with a mixture of fascination and horror. "There is even a strange death-like smell in here."

Jenny said, "You mean like rotting bones?"

"That's it!"

Jenny let out a chuckle. "That's the power of your imagination, honey. I can't smell anything. The odour is in your mind. It is nothing but a figment of your own mental psyche."

With a dramatic wrinkle of my nose, I sniffed then breathed in more deeply. "Guess you are right," I said in a sheepish voice. "Smells more like plastic and cardboard in here."

Jenny opened her arms wide, round face eager. "These bones are nothing but Hollywood skeletons, every one of them."

"What do you mean?"

"Take a close look, honey." She put on her reading glasses and peered into the face of the businessman figure. "See, they all have perfect teeth!"

I turned to look again at the skeleton. Sure enough, its teeth were flawless. Scary looking but pearly white and perfect.

"Some sort of composite material," Jenny said, tapping the businessman's teeth. Then she pointed at another figure, a police officer on a horse. "They are all from a cast."

From somewhere but sounding like it emanated from a mannequin in the room, came a scream.

A terrified wail.

"Booo-hooo-booo!"

I jumped, almost colliding with the businessman.

"Booo-hooo-booo!"

I screamed.

A figure sprang out from behind the mannequin of the coal miner. Its head was covered in a black hood, part of a cloak which extended to the floor, and it carried a scythe in the right hand. "Would you be an angel, and scream like that again? I'd like to add it to my acting repertoire."

"Pete Brown! What on earth are you doing?"

"My job, Doris."

"Since when has jumping out of darkened corners in a black cloak and scaring people been a job?"

"Since I took employment as part of Mr Channer's *Bones in the Night, Ghosts in the Day* exhibition. I'm playing the Grim Reaper. Do you like my interpretation?" Pete tipped back his head and wailed. "Booo-hooo-booo!"

"Oh, for heaven's sake! That's enough." I folded my arms to slow my thudding heart.

Pete adjusted his hood. "The rules are the rules. It's part of Mr Channer's *Spook 'Em* exhibit. Jump and scare is what we are paid to do. Mr Channer wants visitors to experience a visceral response to his art. Just larking about. Fun, isn't it?"

I said, "You almost gave me a seizure."

"The voice-throwing, impersonation, and ventriloquism lessons are paying off. Watch this, Doris."

Pete extended his chin and moved his jaw slowly from side to side like a cow chewing its cud. His eyes closed, mouth opened into a wide oval, and in a voice mimicking Captain Honeybush, he said, "What do you say, Old Gal? booo-hooo-booo!"

Then he rapped the scythe on the floor.

Tap-tap-tap.

"Stop that!" I said. "It's creepy."

"Oh, don't be silly. It's only a lark." Pete rubbed his jaw. "Tonight was a dress rehearsal. Would you believe there are hundreds of shortcuts through this place? I've learned over a dozen. I'm meeting the other actors in the lobby for a debrief. There is another practice tomorrow evening. I'll have perfected my death wail by then."

"The whole thing is ridiculous," groaned Jenny in annoyance. "Where is Mr Channer?"

Pete twisted his mouth into an evil grin. "Buggered off like greased lightning half an hour ago. Doris, you should have joined us. This is easy money!"

I knew he was right. It was better than working as a security guard in a deserted part of the building. "Next time I'll listen to you; that's a promise."

"Make sure you do that. Headed to the archives area, then?" Pete smiled.

"That's right," Jenny said. "Doris is the acting security guard for tonight."

"Might spring a little surprise on you later, then," Pete said with a mischievous twinkle in his eyes. "Something that'll really make you jump."

"Don't you dare do!" I said, glaring at the man. Not that I thought he'd listen; playing tricks was how he got his kicks. In acting class they were fun. I wasn't so sure I felt the same way about his escapades in the museum.

Pete stood there rubbing his chin. "Only a little lark, for my acting repertoire, darling." Whatever devious plot was spinning around his mind, he kept it to himself.

"Come on, Doris," Jenny said, tugging at my arm. "This way to the archives area."

Chapter 15

WITHIN FIVE MINUTES we were in the musty, windowless room that served as the lobby to the archives. Under the semi-dark of the low-wattage night lights, the lifeless space took on an otherworldly aura. Two of I.A. Channer's figures stood like Roman centurions on either side of the reception desk: a basketball player with an ultra-thin body and a yellowed, melon-sized skull for a head and a stooped, old woman holding a feather duster, whose skeleton feet wore no shoes and face was nothing but shade.

"Honey, they've put Mr Channer's figures in here as well." Jenny put on her glasses then fiddled with the old woman's feather duster. "Looks like one my mother used."

"Why are they in here?" The figures put me on edge—especially the old woman who looked like a real-life bag lady. "This area won't be open to the public during the I.A. Channer exhibition, will it?"

"You are right, honey. It won't." Jenny stared at the figures speculatively, as if considering a more suitable answer to my question. "Maybe the museum is using this space as an overflow area."

One or two doubts crept into my mind. "But this room is so far away from the main exhibition, why not store them somewhere else?"

Something I couldn't read flickered in Jenny's eyes. "They must be part of the exhibition, placed here for ambiance."

I shrugged and said, "The basketball player's skeleton fingers are way too large to be real. The whole figure is a monstrous giant, must be seven feet tall, makes me feel claustrophobic."

Jenny nodded in agreement. "Let's make do and mend, honey. In the morning I'll see if they can be moved someplace else."

"That would be a good idea." I glanced from the basketball player to the bag lady with a sense of unease, although I could not pinpoint what troubled my mind. "This place is sinister enough without giant-handed and faceless effigies staring at you."

"Doris, I'm with you on that," Jenny said as she pulled up a chair. "Let me take the weight off my feet."

"Oh, are you staying for a while?" The question came out as a dry-mouthed squeak, and I prayed she'd remain, at least until my nerves stop jangling.

Jenny shot a swift glance at the mannequins and said. "Righto, honey. This is where I'll sit. If you don't mind, I'll hang around with you until your shift is over. At my age sleeping through the night is difficult. I'd rather stay here and chat."

"Thank you," I giggled nervously. "An overnight in a museum archives is not my thing, not too keen on visiting them during the day, either."

Jenny's hazel eyes fixed unwaveringly on mine. "Nothing to fear here." She eased herself down. "The archives area is behind that door. There is the main room and four or five smaller spaces at the back. No need to patrol those: Captain's orders."

"That sounds like a plan," I said, settling into my chair.

"We are supposed to walk around every fifteen minutes," said Jenny. "But once an hour is enough at night. Why don't we just take turns?"

"Anything we need to be on the lookout for?"

"Not really. I suppose you might see a mouse, but other than that it will be quiet. Rodents don't bother you, do they?"

"Oh no, not after meeting Captain Honeybush," I said and laughed. "The critters could run all over me now, and I wouldn't bat an eyelid."

I sank deeper into the chair, crossed an ankle over my knee, and glanced around. Mentally, I went over some topics to talk about to help pass the time. There was the mayhem caused by the Retirees' Spring Festival, the explosion in seagull numbers, and the unusually warm weather.

Maybe we'd get to chat a little about France, not that I could recall much of my school French. Then there were the photographs of Old Betty.

At some point, the conversation would die out, and maybe I'd even get to take a little cat nap. With Captain Honeybush out of the picture, and Jenny at my side, I sensed a rather more relaxing night ahead than I'd first imagined.

Jenny's phone rang.

"Miss Jenny Styles here. Oh, hello... Very well, Nurse.... Really? Are you sure? Oh dear... No, no... Understood... Bye."

There was a tense moment of silence when I heard only the raspy sound of Jenny's breathing as she stared at her phone. After a long moment she looked up, face paled, and in a trembling voice said, "I'm afraid a resident I care for at the Skegness Hospice has taken a turn for the worse. I'm sorry, Doris, but I've got to leave you on your own tonight."

Chapter 16

JENNY STYLES DIDN'T say a whole lot more as she picked up her belongings. It must have been close to midnight as she hurried from the reception area.

I wasn't happy to see her leave.

I felt fretful and skittish as I wondered how I would make it through the night. I glanced at the I.A. Channer mannequins only to become more edgy.

"Should have brought a book to read."

I pulled out the drawer on the desk. On top of a pile of papers lay an old tape cassette and several cassette cases. Quickly I went through the stack—nothing caught my interest. Then I remembered my phone. I scrolled through text messages, pausing to read a note from Grace Rivers:

Hope things are going well.
Joey is sound asleep.
Once again, thank you for being a friend and saving my bacon.
Your number one fan.
Grace.

Ten minutes later I pulled up Facebook. Tonight it didn't hold my attention. Eventually, I started a James Patterson e-book.

But I couldn't settle.

There was something unnerving about the room. And it wasn't just the two mannequins standing either side of the desk. I had the distinct feeling that I was being watched.

I put down my phone and listened.

Nothing.

"Don't be silly, Doris. Only you, the mice, and the mannequins in here tonight."

But the eerie feeling of eyes watching my every move didn't go away.

Again, I glanced around the empty room, eyes eventually settling on the mannequins.

"Damn things are so creepy!"

It was as if the figures were observing me, especially the bag lady, which was crazy because she didn't have a face. Then a thought struck. The basketball player was large enough for someone to... hide in.

Pete Brown's little surprise?

I stood up and walked to the front of the desk. There was certainly enough room in the figure for Pete to squeeze inside. But how had he gotten into the room? Jenny and I were here all the while.

"A shortcut through the museum!"

On the tips of my toes, with hands slightly shaky, I peered up into the face of the basketball player. The yellowed skull was way too large to be human, almost watermelon sized. The teeth were perfect, like the choppers of a Hollywood actor. When I pulled out a pen from my handbag and tapped at them, a hollow clack echoed through the room.

"Nothing in there but moulded plastic."

Now I turned to the bag lady. Her semi-soft skin, greyish-black and dry, appeared to glow in the gloom with weak fluorescence. I reached out a hand and touched the exposed neck. It was rough and cold as if made up of sandpaper. Then I clasped my hand tight around the feather duster and tugged. It didn't move.

"Superglue, and lots of it," I said into the darkness.

The thought of plastic dummies held together by adhesive eased my nerves a little. But I was too on edge to sit down, so I turned to pace the room. At the door that led out to the main area, I swiped at the light switches, hoping to turn up the illumination, but no matter which combination I flipped the light level remained unchanged.

"Must be on a timer," I muttered, pacing back to the desk. Even now, I stood rather than sat as I thought about what to do next. Jenny mentioned patrolling the archives area every hour.

"No time like the present."

Holding the phone tight in my right hand, handbag slung over my shoulder, I moved towards the door to the archives area.

It opened without a sound.

The air was thick with the smell of old paper like the dust that clogs the back of your throat in a second-hand bookshop. I stood blinking for a minute until my eyes adjusted to the gloom.

It was a vast windowless room with wooden desks along the far wall. A central path was crisscrossed by narrow aisles separated by tall metal shelves. The feeble ceiling light gave the place the feel of a hallway in a cheap hotel.

For several moments I glanced around wondering where to begin. Then I walked towards the nearest aisle, where shelves packed with binders, folders, and boxes of all sizes stretched from the floor to the ceiling.

I walked back to the central aisle and headed to the tables at the back of the room. I flipped every light switch I passed. None came on, not even the old fashion desk lamps. Then I strode along the back wall, counting the doors that led to the other storage spaces as I went. There were five doorways each with the words *STAFF ONLY* hand painted in red.

At the final door, I stopped abruptly. There was a definite sense of being observed. I spun around, eyes darting in every direction.

No one.

I stood very still listening. There was no sound of footsteps, no hidden breaths, nothing to suggest anyone else was in the archives.

Finally, I let out a deep sigh.

"Silly billy."

A soft rustle sent a chill skittering up my spine.

Mice?

Frigid air whistled over me.

"Who's there?"

No answer.

Stay calm and use logic.

But I didn't feel calm, and logic wasn't a subject I excelled in.

Another icy blast disturbed a stack of newspapers on a nearby shelf.

I thought of Old Betty.

I thought of Fiona Fenchurch.

And with panicked steps, I hurried from the archives.

Chapter 17

BREATHING FAST AND shallow, unable to slow my thudding heart, I slumped into the chair at the desk in the reception area. Thoughts of fleeing the building sprung to mind. If it were not for the tremble in my legs, I might have carried through with the idea.

How on earth was I going to make it through the night?

There was no choice. I had to call Grace to let her know I'd bailed.

As my breathing became less laboured and my skittering heartbeat eased, I picked up my phone, pressed ON. Mark Twain's quote flickered across the screen:

"Do the thing you fear most and the death of fear is certain."

I couldn't bail on Grace.

I knew I had to see this through.

I looked up at the basketball player and then to the bag lady. They stood motionless on each side of the desk, just as I had left them.

"Nothing but plastic figures!"

That got my logical brain working. If there was an icy breeze in the archives room, it must have come from somewhere.

An open window?

No.

The archives room was windowless. Anyway, it was warm outside, too warm for an icy chill.

Air-conditioning unit?

If Beachside were an American museum, that would have been worth investigating, but here in England, air-conditioning is a rarity, only radiator heating for the chilly winter nights.

There was one other explanation.

One I didn't like.

What was it Jenny had said?

"Nothing but a figment of your own mental psyche."

Could it be that my skittish mind imagined the whole thing?

I considered that possibility for a while.

Yes, I was jumpy.

Yes, this place creeped me out.

But no, it wasn't a figment of my fevered imagination.

So, what did that leave?

I said, "When you have eliminated the impossible, whatever remains, however improbable, must be the truth." It was from a Sherlock Holmes story.

But the only thing left was... Old Betty.

"That's illogical!"

The words made me laugh out loud. Suddenly, I was curious more than fearful. There was something odd about the archives, and now I was determined to figure it out. The blast of frigid air had some natural cause. I'd probably double over laughing when I found it.

"Only one way to get at the truth, Doris," I said in way of encouragement. "Find the source of the breeze and shut it off."

With a renewed determination, I grabbed my handbag, stood up, and strode to the door that led to the archives. Without hesitation, I flung it open and stepped inside.

Chapter 18

THE ROOM LOOKED AS it did earlier. Crowded shelves, dusty files with study desks at the back. I listened for any movement in the shadows, for the soft rustle of scurrying feet, for anything that might cause goose pimples to rise and my heart to quicken.

Silence.

I felt slightly foolish standing there listening. For what? A mechanical sound? A blast of air? A ghost? On the other hand, Jenny had said Old Betty haunted the museum. Not that I'd ever seen a ghost, but the place reminded me of a mausoleum, and I'd read they are full of spooks.

I walked around the darkened periphery of the room. There were no windows, only the five doors that led to smaller storage spaces. Then I weaved between the stacks of shelves, not sure what I was looking for.

Finally, I retraced my steps, stopping outside the fifth door, as I had done earlier. Like the army officer I'd seen at the movies, I did a slow three hundred and sixty degree turn, looking in every direction, including up.

The entire room was silent, motionless.

Baffled, I stared at the door. It was like the others along this wall, a small metal handle with one of those old-fashioned locks that took a long cylindrical key. It sat firm against the wall with no noticeable cracks where a breeze might blow through.

I turned to leave but hesitated. I wouldn't settle until I'd solved the mystery or at least checked off a logical explanation. Without giving myself time to think further, I turned back to the door, reached out a hand, and tugged at the handle.

It swung inward without even a creak.

I hesitated at the entrance, peering into the darkness. My nostrils filled with a mildew tang. The place felt like an unopened tomb. I groped for a light switch and found it. A single low-wattage bulb illuminated the exposed brickwork. Cobwebbed shelves, dusty boxes, rusted cans, and large, battered, wooden containers cluttered the space. On the wall, near the door, hung a small cracked mirror.

"Just a storage room."

I turned to leave, glimpsed something out of the corner of my eye and turned back. On the floor, behind a stack of blackened, wooden crates was a pair of washed-out, orange flip-flops.

But it wasn't the beach footwear that caused me to freeze.

It was the skeleton feet.

I moved closer, heart in my throat.

"Another of Mr Channer's figures!"

I relaxed.

Tap-tap-tap.

The sound came from the main archives. I spun around, crouching low against the shelving.

"Doris, are you in here, Old Gal?"

Chapter 19

JENNY SAID SHE'D PUT a little something in Captain Honeybush's drink. Obviously, that hadn't worked tonight. There was one thing for which I was certain, a man like the captain does not give up easily. *Un gentleman intouchable,* Jenny had called him. A persistent pest, would be a better fit. The thought of his odious leer caused my skin to crawl. I couldn't face him right now. I might say something I'd enjoy but later regret, and Grace would be out of a job.

Tap-tap-tap.

I crouched lower, holding my breath.

There was only one way in and one way out of this storage space.

I was cornered like a crab in a pot.

Forgetting about the mannequin, I scanned for a better place to hide. My feet knew the way, which was a blessing because my mind was in a blind panic. Barely breathing, I listened from behind a stack of large boxes for the sound of the captain's cane striking the concrete floor, or his voice, which tonight sounded reedy and hollow.

Probably the brandy, I thought, as my mind raced for a way out of this mess.

Tap-tap-tap.

I considered calling for help on my mobile phone. But even a whispered voice would alert the captain to my location. He'd be in here before the likes of Constable Wriggly turned over in his bed.

No.

I would wait it out.

I glanced up at the ceiling and let out a soft moan. The storage room bulb flicked in the gloom. Its soft yellow glow would attract the captain's attention like a moth to a streetlamp.

Oh bugger!

With stealth I crept to the door, stopping every few steps to listen. At the wall, I held my breath, and with a trembling hand, flipped the switch. The light went out with a soft hum. Next, I eased the door shut.

Tap-tap-tap.

I sat in the pitch black, and waited.

Chapter 20

IT FELT LIKE AN HOUR but was probably fifteen minutes, when a persistent buzz caused me to jump. The sound came from my handbag. With the skill of an airport baggage screener, I rummaged through the contents, snatching the phone into a shaky hand.

A text message glowed bright in the dark gloom.
Hope everything is going well.
I'm at the hospice, rather bleak I'm afraid.
Captain Honeybush was here when I arrived. For once he is sober! The patient is a friend of his.
Hope all is going well for you there. Any problems, call me.
Jenny.

It took a moment for the meaning to settle in. Then everything became clear, and I was furious. I scrambled forward to flip on the light and marched out of the room.

"Pete Brown!"

The man mentioned he'd left a little surprise for me. Obviously, he was still in the museum, lurking in a dark corner, doubled over with laughter.

"Where are you, Pete? Come out. You've had your fun. Ha. Ha. Ha."

Twice, I walked around the archives calling his name. Then I weaved between the stacks.

No Pete.

Finally, I strode out of the archives back to the reception area.

Chapter 21

PETE BROWN LIKES TO watch his pranks unfold. The man gets a kick observing people's reactions, softening the blow with a friendly smile and his catchphrase, "Just larking about. It's for my acting repertoire, darling."

But Pete wasn't in the archives or the reception area.

That left me puzzled.

I walked to the door that led to the main museum. I peered out into the hallway, half expecting to see Pete doubled over in fits of laughter.

Nothing but exhibit cases.

I stepped fully into the hallway, placing my hands on my hips as I looked in both directions.

"Pete Brown, show yourself, now!"

Silence.

Back at the reception desk, I texted Jenny a message.

I fumed. Fun and games in our acting class were one thing, but this was work. There was no way Pete's game would spook me out, not on my first night standing in for Grace Rivers—not any night for that matter.

As I sat at the desk, my Sherlock Holmes brain began to put the pieces of the puzzle together. Pete had impersonated the captain's voice. The tapping of the captain's cane was easily explained too. He'd used his Grim Reaper's scythe. With the satisfied relief that comes with the completion of a Sunday crossword puzzle, I realized he was lurking in some dark corner ready to spring out and frighten me.

"The trick will be on Pete tonight," I said to the basketball dummy.

But where was Pete hiding?

Then I remembered the figure in the small room at the back of the archives.

"Another of Pete's little spooky tricks?"

They say we vanquish our fears with practise, and that was true for me and the archives. Gone was the earlier feeling of trepidation at being alone with all those dusty shelves and stacks of boxes. In its place was a familiarity, like a pair of well-worn slippers or that favourite black dress for special occasions. I guess it is how an undertaker feels at the sight of yet another dead body. Not fearful, just resigned.

That was how I was feeling as I marched into the archives. At the study desks I paused momentarily to glance around then headed to the door of the fifth storage space.

I pushed the door open and flipped on the light.

Something tapped my shoulder.

I spun around.

"Pete Brown!"

Nothing.

Letting out a little nervous chuckle, I turned back to my task.

Under the single low-wattage light, the bones of the figure's feet seemed almost yellow. The orange flip-flops were well worn, as if they'd walked many miles on sandy beaches.

I moved a box to get a better view.

A skeleton arm flopped, causing a plume of dust to fly in the air.

I stumbled backwards, gasping in the dry particles.

"A little too authentic," I muttered, regaining my footing.

I moved another box. A ragged summer dress, stained with dark splotches, clung to the meagre frame. Carefully I edged around the figure, kneeling down by its head. It was more or less a skull—a gruesome mask of one, though. There were tufts of hair on the scalp, tiny, dark eye sockets and too many teeth.

Goose pimples rose on my arms.

The teeth!

My throat made a dry rasping sound as I scrambled to my feet and ran.

Chapter 22

I SAT IN THE ARCHIVES reception area holding a mug of milky, sweet tea as police officers, crime scene technicians, and paramedics swirled about.

"Take another sip of tea, Mrs Cudlow," Constable Celia Bell said. Her smile showed genuine concern. "Inspector Doxon is on his way, but I'd better get a statement for the record."

I told the constable about my evening, beginning with meeting Fred Faul at the front entrance through to my discovery of the body. I left out the spooky sounds and cold swirls of air.

"I see," Constable Bell said, putting down her pen. "So, you entered the storage room as part of your regular rounds?"

"That's right."

"Do you usually check the storage rooms?"

"First night on the job."

"What were you looking for?"

I shrugged. "I'm not sure. I thought I heard something."

"Really?" Constable Bell picked up her pen.

"But it was nothing." I left Pete Brown out of it, knowing this wasn't one of his tricks.

Constable Bell took me through the statement several times, checking and rechecking facts at various points. Then as two paramedics carried out a stretcher with an impossibly thin black bag on it, she asked, "Mrs Cudlow, is there anything else you'd like to tell me?"

"No," I said, watching the paramedics manoeuvre the stretcher through the reception area and out of the door. "I wonder who it is, and how they got there?"

Constable Bell let out a tired sigh. "From the state of the body, I'd say it has been there quite a while. Doctor Bellamy will tell us more when the test results come in."

"Can't imagine what she was doing in that room," I muttered. "Poor woman."

"What makes you say she?" Constable Bell's eyes narrowed, and she picked up her pen, poised to write. "You seem certain it was a woman."

I considered my response. "The flip-flops, I suppose, and the body was too large to be a child." Then I added with a touch of annoyance. "But I guess it might be a small man who likes to cross-dress."

Constable Bell put down the pen and leaned in close. "Mrs Cudlow, is there anything else you'd like to share before Inspector Doxon arrives?"

It was a question I didn't get to answer.

"Get the hell out of my way!"

Mr Channer stormed into the reception area with an orange bucket and a white spade in his left hand. He wore a black undertaker's suit, black shirt, and black tie. The ribbon on his goatee beard was also black. On his head, at a slight angle, rested an ebony top hat. On the brim, five electronic candles flickered. The man looked like Scrooge from the Charles Dickens' novel, only less friendly.

Constable Wriggly, trailing a pace or two behind the artist said, "Sir, you can't go in there."

"Never have I seen such desecration," barked back Mr Channer, waving the white spade high in the air. "I won't stand for it!"

Constable Wriggly, panting like a dog in the summer heat said, "Only officials allowed in here, sir. Please follow me to the museum lobby." He reached out and took Mr Channer by the arm. "This way, please."

Mr Channer snatched away his arm and spun around to face the police officer. His eyes were wide and wild, dark lips curled back exposing doglike teeth. "Bloody coppers, always causing trouble. Get your filthy hands off me."

Constable Wriggly's eyes bugged as he drew his nightstick.

"That'll be all, Constable," said Inspector Doxon, entering the room. He wore a crumpled, mud-brown suit, cream shirt, and a plum-red tie. His bald head and flat fishlike, unemotional eyes gave him the look of a washed-out college history teacher.

Constable Wriggly backed away. "Right you are, sir."

Inspector Doxon's lips curled up at the edges, his version of a welcoming smile. He said, "Mr Channer, isn't it?"

"That's damn right! What the hell do you think you and your flunkies are doing? The city council won't stand for the desecration of my art. Neither will my adoring fans. If you don't put an end to this madness right now, I'll sue the lot of you."

The inspector kept his voice level. "A security guard discovered a body in the archives area, sir."

"This place is full of bodies. All created by the great artist I.A. Channer." He pointed at himself as he spoke. "Bodies are my business. Scandal and outrage are how I pay the bills."

"We are talking human remains, sir."

There was a long silence.

"Wonderful!" Mr Channer threw his hands in the air. He pressed a button on his hat, the candles flashed in a rhythmic sequence. "This is more than I could have prayed for."

Inspector Doxon licked his lips. "Is that so, sir?"

"Bloody right it is. Is the press here yet? I'd better give a statement." He turned to leave.

The inspector reached out a restraining arm. "Not yet, sir. I have a few questions."

Mr Channer touched the brim of his hat. The candles dimmed. "Who the hell are you anyway?"

"Inspector Doxon, Skegness Police."

"Well, Inspector Doxon, I suggest you sod off."

If his offensive comment surprised the inspector, it didn't show on his face. "Sir, we could always do this down at the station."

Mr Channer twiddled the black ribbon on his goatee beard. "I want to speak to my lawyer."

"That won't be necessary, sir. If you could answer a few—"

"Am I under arrest?"

"No."

"Are you threatening me with arrest?"

The inspector blinked. "No."

"Then sod off."

With that, Mr Channer turned and stormed from the room.

Chapter 23

AN HOUR LATER IN THE main lobby by the desk, under the huge sign that gave the museum's hours of operation, I waited with a small group of museum workers. Captain Honeybush and Jenny Styles arrived together.

The captain hurried to the group, leaning on his cane. Out of breath and visibly sweating, he said, "I hear it was you who found the body; is that correct Mrs Cudlow?"

"That's right," I said, keeping my response short. It was late, and I hoped the captain would send us home.

"A body in a storeroom in the *Lincolnshire Weekly News* archives, Old Gal?"

"Yes, sir. I've given a full statement to the police."

"A statement... to the police?" The captain's face paled.

"That's right." I hesitated, wondering whether to go on. "They may ask for more details later. I told them what I remembered."

The captain's peanut-brown eyes shrunk to tiny dots in his doughy face. His lips curled into a snarl. "Insubordination!"

"Pardon?" I said, stepping back.

Captain Honeybush raised his cane. "I gave express instructions to stay away from the storage areas. I expect my workers to follow my orders to the letter. And now you've spoken to the police without my express permission!" His chin wobbled violently as he spoke. "If you were in the army, I'd have your—"

"Now, now," interrupted Jenny, placing a hand on the captain's arm. "I think congratulations are in order. If it were not for Mrs Cudlow the body might have remained undiscovered for months. She deserves a pay raise for her brave actions."

"Stuff and nonsense," muttered the captain. "I would have found the body on my rounds. I keep a keen eye on all areas under my command."

"Nevertheless, Mrs Cudlow deserves a medal," Jenny said.

Captain Honeybush waved a dismissive hand. "Let us wait to hear what the police have to say before handing out congratulatory praise." He turned to face the small group of overnight workers. "Who worked the last daytime shift?"

Fred Faul shuffled forward. "Did a double shift in the archives, Captain." There was a whiff of cheap alcohol about the man, and his words were somewhat slurred.

The captain didn't seem to notice. "You check the storage rooms regularly, don't you?"

Fred shifted from leg to leg, and his eyes dropped. "Oh yes, I checked the entire archives area at the end of my last shift, sir."

Captain Honeybush rubbed the back of his neck. "Are you sure, old man?"

"Every shift, sir." Fred straightened, pushing out his chest. "If there is talk of a pay rise, it should go to me because checking the storage spaces has become somewhat of a habit, been doing it since I started working here, sir."

The captain shook his cane and barked, "What the devil are you playing at? That is against my express orders."

Fred's shoulders slumped. "Well... I... err... like to be thorough, Captain."

Captain Honeybush twiddled his moustache, his eyes mere slits. "Seems to me things are getting rather slack around here. Maybe it's time for fresh blood; fire the old guard."

Fred shrunk back like a hiker who'd stepped on a snake. "If there was a body in that storeroom, I would have seen it. It wasn't there yesterday. I am certain of that, sir."

But the captain wasn't listening. His face purpled, voice rose to almost a shout. "Mr Faul, how many of my other orders have you wilfully disobeyed?"

"Well... sir... I... err..." Fred glanced in my direction, pointed a gnarled finger, and like a five-year-old deflecting attention from having eaten the last slice of chocolate cake said, "Seems like Mrs Cudlow has unleashed the devils from Hades on us all, and it is only her first night in the museum. Makes you wonder if perhaps she isn't... cursed?"

Captain Honeybush's eyes swivelled in my direction. "You seem to be at the centre of this, Mrs Cudlow. What do you have to say for yourself?"

"That's not fair," Jenny said before my tired mind came out with a crude retort. She placed an arm around my shoulder and in a soft voice said, "Doris, tell everyone what happened, exactly as you told it to the police. That will settle all this nonsense once and for all."

I recounted my story, once again leaving out the spooky bits. When I'd finished, Captain Honeybush said, "The whole situation is rather rum. I'll have to work my network hard to clear up this mess." He tapped the cane several times on the concrete floor as if in deep thought, eyes staring at the ground. When he looked up, there was a shine to his eyes, like a prisoner who'd discovered a secret passage from his prison cell. "If what you say is true, Old Gal, then someone put the body in the storeroom sometime after Fred's last shift."

"But how, and by who?" The question came from Jenny.

"Let us not worry our little minds with such details," boomed Mr Channer as he strolled into the lobby. He pushed a small wooden crate, no larger than a small child. Four candles on the brim of the artist's hat blazed white. There was no light emitting from the fifth candle. "Now is not the time for questions or understanding. Now is the time to give thanks and rejoice!"

"What the dickens are you talking about?" huffed Captain Honeybush.

Mr Channer's dark lips tugged into a fox-like grin. "Ladies and gentlemen, the press will be all over this story. Can you imagine the headlines? The crowds will flock in from all over Lincolnshire, now. I may have to hire more actors to help spook up my artwork." He tipped back his head and cackled like a hyena after the kill. "It's been a long hard road, but now I'm poised to break through to the big league: London, Paris, New York, Beijing. Nothing will stop me now."

Fred grunted then said, "That's if they don't shut the place down. I reckon the board of directors will cancel your exhibition."

Mr Channer took off his hat, ruffled his hair, cursed, and wheeled the wooden crate back and forth. The wheels squeaked as if in protest of their cargo. "They can't do that; I'm an artist!"

"Me too," Fred muttered. "Did I ever tell you about my story of Mr Plum and Mrs Apple? It won the—"

"Shut up! I need to think," yelled Mr Channer.

For half a minute or so, nobody spoke. But I had the distinct sense that Mr Channer was looking at me. His head was tilted to the ceiling, yet I could feel his eyes resting on my face, watching me out of narrowed slits.

With the smooth movement of a cat, his head swung around, he walked towards me, placed an arm about my shoulder. There was a peculiar odour about the man. It clung in the air close to his body as if it emanated from his skin. It was a familiar smell—pickle like, unpleasant, and nauseatingly strong, but I wasn't sure where I smelled it before. Preservative? New furniture? Fresh glue? Or was it the hallway of the Skegness General Hospital mortuary?

Mr Channer said, "So you found the bones, eh?"

"That's right. I've given the police a statement." I eased away from his overpowering scent.

"How very convenient of you," Mr Channer replied, his voice as soft as a whisper. After a long moment, as if practising lines at a dress rehearsal, he said, "This is a sad day for everyone. For the sake of the victim's memory, I shall struggle on with the exhibition. It won't be easy, but the show must go on!"

Chapter 24

WITH RELIEF, I STEPPED out of the entrance of the Beachside Museum and hurried through the early morning dark down the steps to the door of my ancient Nissan Micra. It was crazy that even at 2 a.m. in Skegness the temperature held in the mid-seventies.

I stopped to gaze at the flashing lights of the emergency vehicles. There were four police cars at the front entrance and a forensic truck parked at an angle by a wheelchair-accessible side ramp. Then like a dog shaking off excess water after swimming in a lake, my body gave a shudder. I took a deep breath. The tang of the salt sea breeze felt like oxygen must to a deep-sea diver.

"Doris, you made it through the night—just!"

The engine growled into life at the first flick of the key: not precisely a purr, more like the rattle and chug of a diesel locomotive. With care, I glanced in my rear-view mirror, backed out of the parking spot, and pulled out of the car park onto the main road.

A red light flashed on the dashboard—low fuel.

"Oh bugger!"

Any other night I would have ignored it. Daytime, when there were people about, was my preferred time to refuel. I find most petrol stations at night unsettling. After dark is when the cash-and-grab merchants stalk their prey; when the shotgun carrying robbers make their strike.

I was still considering what to do when I saw the bright lights of Skegs Stop. It is the safest place in town to refuel after hours. A couple close to retirement, George and Mildred Seeton, run the station. Mildred is one of Mrs Lintott's bingo ladies, and George is a know-it-all handyman who enjoys the occasional flutter at Bet Quick Bookies on Ida Road.

Bright lights illuminated the pumping area. Their brilliant luminance soothed my jangled nerves. A plastic packet blew across the empty forecourt as I stepped out of the car. The air filled with a mixture of petrol, oil, and diesel.

With an unconscious movement I swiped my credit card. The fuel gurgled into the tank as my eyes focused on the dial. Three pounds was my limit tonight. Lost in the events of the past few hours I did not register the hurried footsteps until a male voice said, "Mrs Cudlow, that you?"

I jumped.

"Sorry, didn't mean to scare you." George raised both hands, palms out. He was a large, shambling man with a sharp nose, gapped teeth, narrow squinting eyes, and pointed pixie ears. Tonight, he wore his usual uniform, baggy, brown corduroy trousers with a faded, blue *Skeggy Stop* shirt that stretched taut across his pot belly. "Heard you were working the Beachside Museum this evening as a security guard. Spot o' bother over there?"

I didn't want to talk about my evening, nor did I want to be the source of town gossip. "Things were under control when I left." It was a hedged answer.

"Just that I saw the flashing, blue lights and wondered what happened. Inspector Doxon stopped by to top up his tank. Rarely see him this time of night, so I figured it was serious." George paused expectantly. When I didn't answer, he pointed with his chin towards the Beachside Museum. "I wouldn't work in that place if they paid me."

I said, "It is a little boring, not much different from working at a petrol station, I suppose."

"For you, maybe, but I'm a local. I know the stories."

I eased the pressure on the pump handle, the dial clicked to five pounds. "What stories?"

"Nothing, Mrs Cudlow. I'm not one for scaring the ladies with silly tales, especially at this time in the early morning. Not good for business." George shook his head as if clearing his mind. "I hear pandemonium broke out in the *Lincolnshire Weekly News* archives section tonight. Haven't got all the details, yet. That's not the area where you patrolled, is it?"

I placed the handle back in the petrol pump as I considered my answer. "What makes you ask?"

George rubbed a thick hand through his hair and glanced over his shoulder. "Listen, I've got a little flutter on with the postie... the exhibits... nothing happened... I mean you didn't break anything, did you?"

Rather than get annoyed, I changed the subject to give him something else to gossip about. "The police found a body in the *Lincolnshire Weekly News* archives section of the museum."

To say George's eyes grew wide is an understatement. The squinty orbs opened: melon sized. "A real body?"

"Yep."

George rubbed a hand on his neck. "Wait till I tell Mildred. She'll never believe it." He turned, gazing off towards the Beachside Museum. "Man or woman?"

"Sorry, I'm not an expert in skeletons. But I think it was a woman."

George's mouth opened into an O. With his wide eyes, gapped teeth, and pixie ears, he looked like a braying donkey. "Skeleton? Oh my God, it's Fiona Fenchurch!"

I said, "The woman at the centre of the Dancing Hands Mystery?"

He nodded mutely. But it was the certainty in his eyes that convinced me of his belief.

I said, "We can't be sure. The police are investigating as we speak."

George leaned against the petrol pump to steady himself. "They say she always returns what she takes."

"Who?"

"Old Betty, the Beachside Museum ghost."

Chapter 25

IT WAS CLOSE TO 3 A.m. when I parked the Nissan Micra in the street outside of Whispering Towers Boarding House. A bright yellow moon shone from a star-filled sky. Besides the faint rustling of a sea breeze through tree branches, the street was silent. Even the light in Mrs Lintott's kitchen window was out.

"Thank goodness she is sound asleep," I muttered as I locked the car door. The last thing I needed after the gruelling night was a long, rambling chat with the landlady. That would happen in the morning, as soon as she got up and her phone rang. What I wanted was a shower, fresh clothes, thinking time, and sleep.

The first three were easy. I wasn't sure about the forth.

The familiar smells of the darkened hallway washed over me like a foam-filled bubble bath. I relaxed then made my way, on tip-toes, up the stairs to my bedsit apartment door. For a moment I paused, half expecting, even at this late hour, to see Mrs Lintott scampering along the hall with her familiar cry of *Yoo hoo, Doris*. But no doors creaked open; there was no call from the bottom of the stairs.

With a deep sigh, I put the key in the lock and turned. I've no idea why I do that. The lock doesn't work. I guess it is just a habit.

At the kitchen table, I hung the jacket on the back of the chair, placed the security guard cap on the table and sipped a glass of water, too tired to rise for my shower. I needed something stronger, like a splash or two of Mrs Lintott's medicinal brandy to get me going. But a drop would become two or three. Soon, I'd have downed half a bottle. Drink is my nemesis, something I've struggled with since before my marriage to Toby.

I'm an alcoholic, recovering, but bound for life under that curse.

Then there are the pills, sleeping and pain killers mainly. They warn you on the labels they can be addictive. In my case, that is true.

The mobile phone rang.

I jumped, picked up, then chided myself for not noting the number first.

"Captain Honeybush here. Mrs Cudlow, I got your details from the records. How are you doing, Old Gal?"

Oh bugger! Not now. I kept my voice civil, although I felt like cursing. "Is anything the matter?"

"Nothing out of the ordinary, I suppose. Just doing my managerial duty... checking up on you... a single woman... all alone... Whispering Towers Boarding house, isn't it?"

I resisted the urged to slam down the phone. I didn't want to cause any trouble for Grace. I'd made it through the evening and wasn't going to throw it all away because of a bothersome telephone call. "I see. Captain, it is rather late. Thank you, I am fine."

"Like to do it with all my female staff—check-up, that is." He spoke slowly, methodically, as if with each word he was performing a delicate operation.

"I'm turning in for the night. Goodnight."

"Just a quick question, Old Gal." There was an undertone of urgency in his voice.

"Yes, what is it?" I couldn't hide my irritation.

"About the body?"

I became instantly alert. "Yes?"

"Must have given you rather a nasty shock, Old Gal."

"Not the thing you expect to find hidden in a storeroom in a museum."

The captain snorted. "Military officers are trained to expect the unexpected, but I understand your surprise." There was a moment of silence, followed by a sharp intake of breath. "Did the police say anything about... suspects or the like?"

"Suspects?"

"You know, they have a special term for it—persons of interest."

"No."

"Any mention of how she died?"

"She?"

After a long silence, the captain said, "You mentioned it was a woman, didn't you?"

I didn't think so, but tiredness filled my mind with muddle. "Did I really?"

"Yes, you did! I am quite sure, Old Gal. This thing has been rather a shock to your feminine system. Yes... Yes, you told everyone it was a woman. Orange flip-flops, little summer dress, I recall it as if I were there with you. A little shell shock, that's what you are experiencing right now."

For once, I agreed with the pompous man. It had been a trying few hours. I was shattered and a little shell shocked. "Yes, you might be right about that."

"Sleep won't come easy tonight, Old Gal."

Once again, the captain was spot on. "Maybe I'll watch a movie."

"Mrs Cudlow, to tell you the truth, I don't think I can get my head down either." His voice dropped to a throaty growl. "How about I drive over to your place, only take me five minutes, and we share a nightcap over that movie? Whispering Towers Boarding House, top floor, I believe?"

I hung up.

Annoyed and forgetting about Mr Pandy, I stomped to the tiny bathroom. Now I was ready for a shower.

Thud, thud, thud.

"Sorry, Mr Pandy, got to wash away the grime from the day."

I rent an upper-floor room. Mr Pandy rents the room below. The walls are paper-thin, the floorboards squeak, and whenever I use the bathroom the flush echoes like a steam train in a tunnel, a fact Mr Pandy reminds me of by tapping his National Health Service walking stick on his ceiling. If I walk around my apartment late at night or too early in the morning, he does the same.

Thud, thud, thud.

"It's been a challenging day," I yelled. "Have you ever worked in a spooky museum overnight and found a dead body?"

Thud, thud, thud.

I stood for much longer than usual under the steaming water. It did little to wash away the vivid images of my discovery in the Lincolnshire newsroom archives. They came back as the spray splashed against my face. The body was almost skeletal, the summer dress little more than a tattered sheet, but the skull seared the deepest into my psyche. Those ragged tufts of hair and the crooked, yellow teeth.

Chapter 26

I STILL FELT ON EDGE after towelling down and changing into a silk nightdress. At the window, I pushed the curtains aside. A white moon shone in a clear black sky. No sign of a break in the Mediterranean-like weather, just yet. A streetlight flickered, bathing the parked vehicles in a zebra-like streak.

A movement in the shadow caught my eye.

A man?

Captain Honeybush?

I drew back to the side of the frame and peeked around the edge blinking. Something large and shadowy moved beside a van. As if sensing my gaze, it stopped, crouched low, and faded into the dark.

I waited.

The darkness of the street left me uneasy. I thought I heard the tap-tapping of an irritated cane but knew it was nothing more than my vivid imagination.

Still I waited, without movement, peering down into the street.

After a short while, the darkness flickered and a large grey cat hurried out of the shadow, glanced around, and darted away.

I let out an exhausted breath. "Just a figment of my jittery imagination!"

The mobile phone buzzed.

Tense and anxious, I glanced at the screen before answering—Grace Rivers.

"Doris, I can't believe you found a woman's body on my shift. What on earth happened?"

After recounting the evening, I said, "Don't blame yourself. It was random chance. How is Joey?"

"Doing well, but his temperature is still a little high." Grace paused and began to sob. After a moment she regained her composure and continued. "It is difficult raising children as a single parent... I don't know what I'd have done tonight without you."

"That's what friends are for. Happy to do it again, if needed." But my brain hurt at the thought of another shift at the Beachside Museum, and I hoped it wouldn't be necessary.

"Oh no! I don't want to impose."

"Are you sure? It is no trouble." I held my breath.

"That eases my mind," Grace said. "Staying with my son was the best option, but I'll be right as rain for work now."

"Wonderful!" The single word came out like a gasp of relief. If I ever revisited the Beachside Museum, it would be during the day, as a visitor with lots of friends surrounding me, and I'd stick to the gift shop in the main lobby. "It was my pleasure to help you out. Who knows, I might even pick up a shift or two as a security guard." But not at a museum, I added silently.

After a lengthy pause, Grace said, "The thing is, to stay at home with a sick child equals no pay. That's a decision single parents often face. With all of my bills I wasn't sure whether to take time off or—"

I interrupted and said, "You did the right thing. I read in an article that children can take a sudden turn for the worse at any moment. Imagine if something had happened to Joey; you'd never be able to live with yourself." My voice slowed to that of a teacher sounding out a difficult word. "Joey needed his mother."

The line went quiet for so long I thought Grace had hung up. When she spoke her voice was low and serious. "Doris, you always make me think; that's what I like about you..."

"Go on."

"I've got a big favour to ask."

"Uh-huh." I adjusted the phone.

"Can you take my shift tonight?"

"Eh!" My eyes darted wildly around the room, settling on the Beachside Museum security guard cap on the kitchen table. "Go back to the museum?"

"Doris, you are right. I need to be at my child's side, at least until he is a little better." As if sensing my hesitation, Grace added. "There'll be other security guards around; you won't be alone. Anyway, after finding a body, what else could go wrong? Please say yes."

Dear God, I thought but said, "Oh Lord... if you are... sure." Then thinking ahead and hoping for a miraculous recovery of Joey before tonight, I added, "Doctor Bellamy, is he visiting later?"

"No."

"What about the district nurse?"

"The National Health Service is not what it once was."

"Oh!" I sucked in a deep breath. In an unsteady voice I said, "Doris Cudlow at your service."

Words of gratitude tumbled out like water bursting through a dam. "Oh Doris, you are a true friend... that job is our lifeline; without it I'd be lost in debt... this month it will be a tight financial squeeze... not sure how I'm going to pay the bills. I'll cross that bridge later. Once again, thank you, Doris."

Grace hung up.

Breathless, with a headache brewing, I closed my eyes. Then I buried my head in my hands and sat for some time, thinking hard. I couldn't be mad at Joey for being sick or for Grace for asking for help. I couldn't even be mad at myself for wanting to pick up the phone and call back to say no.

But I was mad, anyway.

I'd rather be anywhere else in the world than working the overnight shift at the Beachside Museum under the lecherous gaze of Captain Honeybush and surrounded by spooky objects. And I knew I would have to do that because there was no one else for Grace to turn to.

Furtive footsteps sounded from the stairs.

An authoritative thump rattled the door.

My eyes jerked open in surprise.

The handle turned, and the door swung slowly open.

Chapter 27

"YOO HOO, DORIS, EVERYTHING okay?" Mrs Lintott bustled into the room. She carried a tray with two steaming mugs, and a six-pack of beer. "I heard Mr Pandy banging and thought I'd better check."

"Mrs Lintott, you've got to get my door lock fixed," I snapped. "Anyone could walk in here."

"Yes, love. The lock is at the top of my list, once I've got next month's rent from you. Money doesn't grow on trees. Oh, the cans of beer are a gift from your friend, Grace Rivers."

I fell silent for a moment and then said, "Sorry, Mrs Lintott, it has been a very challenging twenty-four hours."

With light steps, almost skipping, she hurried to the kitchen, put the cans in the fridge and took a seat at the kitchen table.

I waited for a moment to hear Mr Pandy's walking stick.

Only the low buzz of the refrigerator.

As if reading my thoughts, Mrs Lintott winked and said, "Doris, I know every floorboard in this place and where not to step."

That lifted my mood. "You must teach me. I'll do anything to keep Mr Pandy's walking stick at bay."

We both laughed.

"Hot chocolate?" Mrs Lintott picked up a mug from the tray. "I read in the *Sun* newspaper that an ancient tribe in Peru used it as a truth serum. Don't know if it works, but it'll sooth your nerves, help you relax, and ease your sleep."

Grateful, I blew on the surface. "Ahh, I think you're right." I took a long sip. "Just what the doctor ordered."

Mrs Lintott smiled, took a bird sip from her own cup and said, "Doris, I will not ask you about the skeleton you discovered in the Beachside Museum archives."

The speed at which gossip travelled to Mrs Lintott's ears was nothing short of astounding.

"You've heard about it already, then?"

"Oh yes, love. But let's not talk about any of it, tonight. What you need is rest and sleep. Don't let that hot chocolate go cold. It's my grandmother's special mix."

"Thank you," I replied, taking a long gulp and feeling better. I didn't want to talk about the body in the archives but could scarcely believe neither did Mrs Lintott. "Are you feeling okay?"

Mrs Lintott half closed her eyes and continued as if I hadn't spoken. "There is no point raking over old memories, might give you the terrors, and you'd never get to sleep. No, no, that wouldn't be right, not after the long exhausting day you've experienced." Her eyes snapped open. "That's why I brought you the hot chocolate, to help you relax."

"Very thoughtful," I said, waiting for her to continue.

Mrs Lintott picked up the security guard cap, examined it for a moment, and placed it back on the table. "Anyway, Mildred, from the Skeggy Stop, called. She's a real busybody, wouldn't want her as my sister. The woman gave me a blow-by-blow account of everything you told George. No point raking over old ground. Take another sip of your hot chocolate, love. Relaxing, isn't it?"

"Indeed, it is," I said, taking another gulp. "So, Mildred gave you all the details, then?"

"Yes, love. Let's not talk about it. How is the hot chocolate?"

"Lovely." If Mrs Lintott didn't want the details, there was something else she wanted to know. I just couldn't figure out what. I took a mouthful of hot chocolate and said, "Did George tell you his theory on the identity of the body?"

"Oh yes, love." Mrs Lintott brought her mug to her lips but didn't drink. "Doris, you discovered the body of Fiona Fenchurch."

I said, "That's what George reckons." But I wasn't convinced, yet. "Let's wait and see what the police make of it before jumping to any conclusions."

Mrs Lintott tapped the side of her nose. "The bingo ladies have a way of putting two and two together. As sure as eggs are eggs it is Fiona Fenchurch."

"How do you know that for sure?"

"Can't reveal my sources, love, but my phone's been ringing off the hook."

I sat back in my chair and gazed reflectively at Mrs Lintott. "Are you telling me I discovered the body of the woman who was dragged into the sea by Old Betty?"

Mrs Lintott nodded, all slow like she was in an action replay at the Olympics. "That's right, love. I wonder, was there lots of seaweed?"

"Seaweed?"

Mrs Lintott opened her eyes wide. "Surrounding the body of Fiona Fenchurch. I supposed it'd be all dried out, but did you see any?"

A small town like Skegness is always a swirl with unreliable rumours. I wasn't about to add to the speculation, so I said, "I refuse to believe the gossip of your bingo ladies, not without formal confirmation from the police. Fiona Fenchurch disappeared from the beach years ago. How could her body end up in the museum? No, Mrs Lintott, it must be someone else. I bet the Skegness police files are loaded with missing people."

"I'll take the bet: ten pounds?"

Not that I could afford it but I said, "Deal!"

Mrs Lintott's lips curved into a faint tolerant smile and she said, "What we bingo ladies haven't been able to figure out is what happened to the other bodies?"

"Pardon?"

"Mildred put me onto her husband at the end of our chat. He was all of a panic."

"About what?"

"Doris, you didn't break any of I.A. Channer's figures, did you?"

Chapter 28

WHEN THE ALARM RANG, the bedside clock said it was three in the afternoon, a fact confirmed by the bright stream of sunlight flooding through the bedsit window. Groggy, I said, "What on earth did Mrs Lintott put in that hot chocolate?"

I stumbled out of bed, made a coffee, checked my phone for messages, watched silly cat videos on YouTube, then clicked on a link that led to Facebook posts.

"Only ten minutes to catch up on what people are saying," I said to the empty room.

A lengthy article posted by Pete Brown explained why the body I found in the Beachside Museum was that of Old Betty. A comment by a Miss Emily Johnson doubted they wore orange flip-flops back in Old Betty's day. Another comment pointed out the housekeeper's grave in the old rectory cemetery lay undisturbed. A photograph of a tombstone surrounded by overgrown rose bushes confirmed the observation.

George, from Skeggy Stop, posted an image of an angry sea parting, with a stooped, old lady in black dragging a terrified woman dressed in a little summer dress and orange flip-flops into the frothy depths. The text underneath the image said it came to him in a dream, and he wondered if he should share it with the local constabulary.

It had three hundred and forty-seven likes.

There was also a related post by the postie. He'd opened a new book and was taking wagers on Fiona Fenchurch being the first Skegness alien abduction. Her skeleton remains were, so the postie claimed, returned to Earth after devious extra-terrestrial experimentation.

The first like was from anonymous user Wriggly4Detective.

I.A. Channer left a comment which stated they'd be snatching the children next and putting their bodies on display in his exhibition.

I closed Facebook.

I'd just wasted two hours.

"Nothing but gossip, rumour, and speculation." The only thing everyone agreed on was that the body was that of a woman, and even that wasn't a confirmed fact—yet.

The rest of the evening I pottered around. I tidied the kitchen, cleaned the bathroom, and sat down to read a novel. All the while I kept my thoughts away from my upcoming return to the Beachside Museum.

Chapter 29

THE DASHBOARD CLOCK said it was a little before nine forty-five when I pulled my car into a parking space at the front of the Beachside Museum. It was dark and still, the only sound was the distant roar of waves breaking on the shore. Gone were the flashing, blue lights, the emergency vehicles, and men and women in uniform bustling about.

It was as if nothing had happened.

Things were back to normal. Well, besides my thudding heart, which seemed to beat faster every time my thoughts drifted to the upcoming overnight shift.

The urgent shuddering of my mobile phone brought me back to the present. I glanced at the screen before picking up and said, "Hello, Mrs Lintott. Is everything okay?"

"Oh yes, love. Are you driving?" There was something urgent in her voice.

I straightened. "I just pulled into the Beachside Museum car park."

"Then you are sitting down?"

The question caused my heart to beat even faster. It was the suggestion a doctor makes before delivering unwelcome news. "What's happened?"

Mrs Lintott's voice rose an octave. "Oooh, Doris, I was just on the phone with Mrs Symons, one of my bingo ladies. She cleans the police station. Do you know her?"

I'd met Mrs Symons once or twice. The woman was a wellspring of gossip, nearly always more smoke than fire. "Sixty something with brown eyes and shockingly white hair?"

"That's her!" There was a pause as if Mrs Lintott was planning her words. "Mrs Symons called to say they have identified the body."

I pressed the phone hard to my ear. "Really? Who is it?"

"Oooh, Doris, you won't believe it." Mrs Lintott's voice rose to a triumphant squeal. "It is Fiona Fenchurch, after all, just like I told you!"

There was an expectant pause, and I knew she was waiting for me to apologise.

I said, "Sorry for doubting you and your bingo friends. It is just that—"

"We ladies have been around the block a few times, love. We know our eggs from our bacon! I'll add the ten quid on to next month's rent, okay?"

"Ten quid, for what?" Then I remembered our bet and said, "Want to double down?"

"Oh no, love. I know when I'm ahead. To tell you the truth, I wouldn't have believed it myself if I didn't speak with Nurse Phillips. You know her, don't you? Nice lady, works for Doctor Bellamy."

I closed my eyes, trying to visualise the woman. At last I said, "No, I don't believe we have met."

"Well, it doesn't matter, love." Mrs Lintott spoke in a whisper. "Please keep this to yourself. Nurse Phillips says they haven't been able to identify the skeleton from medical or dental records, just yet."

In an unconscious gesture, I adjusted the phone, moistened my lips, and said, "So how can anyone be sure it is Fiona Fenchurch?"

"They found her driving licence with the body."

"All right," I conceded. "I guess the authorities matched Fiona's photograph?"

"No, love. It was one of those old British licences, green, no photograph. Might have been before your time. They issued me one when I began driving, still have it somewhere."

Something was off, but I wasn't sure what. "So, how do they know the body is Fiona?"

The question opened the floodgates. Words flowed out of Mrs Lintott's lips like water rushes along the Mississippi. "Oooh, Doris, Constable Wriggly confirmed the dress and flip-flops matched Fiona's on the day of her disappearance. It beggars belief that a person can disappear on a crowded beach and show up ten years later on display in a museum. Oh my goodness, they say Fiona's neck was 'snapped like a Christmas turkey.' Those are Doctor Bellamy's words. Poor lamb!"

"Broken neck!" I gasped.

"Snapped fully in half as if someone with massive hands grasped and squeezed!" Mrs Lintott was in her element now. Her gossip-filled voice squeaked with the joy of a rabbit let loose in a field of lettuce. "Can't think of who'd have hands that large, except maybe a basketball player. I hear Inspector Doxon has spoken with the chief of Lincolnshire police. Oh Mamma Mia! The chief shouted and cursed then ordered Inspector Doxon to do something before it's all over the national press. Heaven only knows it doesn't look good when the only line of investigation involves a ghost dragging the body into the sea, especially when a police officer guarded it. Dear Lord, the chief called the whole incident an 'embarrassment.' Oh my word, and the postie says he'll open a book and is taking bets on alien abduction. I wonder whether to have a little flutter on—"

I interrupted and said, "Mrs Lintott, are you quite sure of that fact?"

"Which one, love? There are so many; it's a job keeping up."

"About Inspector Doxon meeting with the chief."

"Yes, love. I got it from near the horse's mouth."

There was more; I could sense it, so I said, "The Dancing Hands Mystery was such a long time ago. Do you have any idea what the chief asked Inspector Doxon to actually do?"

"Oooh, yes, but keep it to yourself, love." Mrs Lintott lowered her voice to a conspiratorial whisper. "The chief told Inspector Doxon to reopen the Fiona Fenchurch missing person file and treat it as a cold-case murder investigation. But how they'll arrest the ghost of Old Betty is beyond me."

Chapter 30

AFTER I HUNG UP, I sat in the car, gazing out of the windscreen towards the entrance of the museum. It was dark and still, only the shadows flickered under a weak, streaky moonlight. The news from Mrs Lintott wasn't entirely surprising. But that the Skegness police had opened a murder investigation left me jumpy.

A little blast of classical music would help with relaxation. I clicked the seat belt off, flipped on the radio, and twiddled with the dial:

...body in the Beachside Museum has been identified as that of longtime missing Skegness resident Fiona Fenchurch. She disappeared over ten years ago in what has become known as the Dancing Hands Mystery. Expect the warm weather to continue for a day or two. Now, we interrupt our Classical Classics show to bring you Skegness FM 87.7 breaking news. The Skegness Police Department have...

I flipped off the radio.

Sucking in a long breath, I let the air out gradually.

"One... Two... Three..."

Deep breathing always works to calm down my thoughts when I'm stressed. As I counted, I visualised how the evening would go. In my mind, I sat content, chatting to Jenny Styles in the little reception area outside of the *Lincolnshire Weekly News* archives.

"Four... Five... Six..."

Our conversation would naturally include the latest Facebook posts about the murder investigation along with gossip about police suspects.

"Seven... Eight... Nine..."

Then we'd walk the archives, together. Later, seated back at the reception desk, I'd start on a light-hearted P.G. Woodhouse novel. Then, with nothing much happening, I'd jot down a few notes for my article on Old Betty, with Jenny's insights fuelling one of the best pieces I've written.

"Ten."

My heartbeat slowed, mind cleared, and the lingering doubts vanished.

"I can do this."

I pumped a fist in the air. I'd already worked one shift in the museum. With the reading, conversation, and note taking, the shift would fly by.

"I'm ready!"

The mobile phone vibrated—a text message from Jenny.

Doris, hope you've recovered from yesterday. What a thing to find on your first night in the archives. It would have sent me batty!

But you are young and resilient. At my age, a shock like that takes days to recover from. I'm sure you understand. And with events at the hospice, my nerves are all a jangle.

All that to say I won't join you at the museum tonight. I'm sure you can handle anything that comes up.

Regards,
Miss Jenny Styles

"Oh bugger!"

I read and re-read the text, each time hoping miraculously the words would take on another meaning.

They didn't.

After the fifth read-through and acting with no conscious effort on my part, my hand flipped the ignition key, and I backed the car out of the parking space.

"No!" I shouted at my body, which seemed to have decided it wasn't spending the night in the Beachside Museum. "I'm doing this for Grace and Joey."

And anyway, I thought, as my mind took back control of my limbs, Grace was right, after last night what else could possibly happen?

I pulled the car forward, turned off the ignition, climbed out, and hurried to the entrance, determined not to give my body time to object.

The main door flew open. A whirl in a crumpled suit knocked me to one side.

"Whoa!" I reached out to a handrail to steady myself. "You almost ran me over!"

"Sorry, sorry. I've got to get out of here." The voice screeched like fingernails on a blackboard.

Then the night air filled with the whiff of cheap alcohol, and recognition set in. I said, "Fred Faul! What in heaven's name is the matter with you?"

Fred's face seemed translucent under the dim entranceway lights, but his eyes were alive, alert, and opened very wide. "Mrs Cudlow, you can have my damn shift, every last one of them."

I wasn't sure how to respond to Fred's outburst. "What happened?"

Fred's mumbled words were the only thing that could have stunned me more than seeing him flee in a blind panic from the building. "A pack of rabid dogs couldn't drag me back into that place."

"Eh?"

"I've quit." He kept moving towards the car park as he spoke.

Fred wasn't known for his work ethic. Jobs that required minimal effort attracted him like a bee to honey. If Fred quit, it was because they'd asked him to do actual work. "For heaven's sake, what are you trying to escape from, now?"

"Old Betty... I saw her!"

Chapter 31

IT TOOK EVERY OUNCE of willpower not to turn around and follow after Fred. Part stubbornness, part curiosity, and part determination not to let Grace Rivers down kept me going.

Trying to be invisible as possible, I walked into the lobby and eased myself between a small huddle of people crowded around the reception desk. They were the actors hired by Mr Channer to "spook up" his exhibition, each outfitted in ghostly apparel. I recognised a few faces from my Tuesday evening acting class. Everyone spoke in hushed tones. It felt like an all-too-real version of Halloween.

There was only one other person in a security uniform. A lanky man with a lazy slouch who I didn't recognize. Attached to his jacket, at a lopsided angle, his name badge read Tony Pigro. He leaned on the edge of the reception desk, eyes half closed, as if he'd rather be tucked up in bed. I glanced at his jacket pocket and saw it bulged with a rum bottle and wondered if he might be slightly drunk. If anything happened tonight, I sensed he'd run, but in the opposite direction. That's if he woke up.

The empty chair at the reception desk reminded of Fred's absence.

I took in a halting breath.

Maybe I shouldn't have come here.

"Now listen up," said Captain Honeybush as he jabbed his cane in the air. He looked around the gathered crowd then snatched a sly glance straight at me. "This evening I'm a man down. Our usual night-time reception security guard... err... had to... err... leave early."

"He claimed to have seen a ghost," said a stout woman with frowning eyes. She wore a black, ankle-length, hooded robe, and her dark hair was cut almost to a bristle at the back. "Right here in the museum."

"Where?" The question came from a short, skinny man with a bald head and protruding eyes. A long, black cape hung like a loose curtain off his frame. In his left hand he carried a mannequin's head daubed with red splotches.

"In the *Lincolnshire Weekly* archives section," said the stout woman. "That's where they discovered a body yesterday evening."

The skinny, short man's protruding eyes jutted out farther. "Not going near there, no matter how much Mr Channer is paying."

"Best we spook people where it is not so spooky," agreed the stout woman.

"Stuff and nonsense!" The captain tapped his cane on the floor. "There are no spooks in this museum except you actors."

"But what if something happens?" said the short, skinny man.

"I'm fully trained for any medical emergency, the armed forces, you know. He who dares and all that. Nothing can surprise an old military man. I'll be on duty and by your side at the first sign of trouble." Captain Honeybush paused. "Tonight is your final dress rehearsal, so let's not be having any of this haunting nonsense. Now, who amongst you are ready to earn a few pounds?"

"Yes, yes. Show me the money!" A man dressed as a seagull with thick feathered boards for wings twirled in a circle. "This outfit didn't come cheap, but for thirty pounds an hour, it's well worth it."

There was a general murmur of excited agreement.

The captain raised a palm for quiet. "It appears Mr Channer is running late. He will join us shortly. While we await his arrival, I'm in charge. Questions?"

Before anyone replied, the entrance door swung open.

A stooped figure in a black cloak hurried in.

A hood covered the head, and the person carried a scythe in the right hand. Taking little, fast steps, their shoes clacked on the concrete floor like the clogs of an Irish dancer. But it was the enormous wheeze that caused everyone to look up.

"Sorry I'm late," huffed Pete Brown, flipping the hood off his head. "The wife's not with me tonight, spoke with Fred Faul in the car park, now she's gone back home!"

The captain's face reddened. "Fred Faul! That man enjoys the spirits rather too much, and I'm not talking about the ghostly variety. Damn inebriated fool was always seeing things. I should have let him go years ago. Too soft hearted, that's my problem." He twiddled his moustache and tapped his cane on the floor. "Fall in with your fellow actors."

Pete, always dramatic, doubled over to catch his breath. Resting an arm on the captain, he took exaggerated gasps until he was sure all eyes were on him. When he straightened, there was a slight curl at the edges of his lips, and his face was ghastly white.

"Are you all right, old man?" The captain's anxious voice broke the tension. "Not a heart attack is it, old bean?"

Pete spread his arms wide and swayed from side to side.

Captain Honeybush's face paled. "My God, is there a medical practitioner amongst us?"

Pete clasped his hands on his chest, staggering backwards.

"Lord, someone call for an ambulance," squealed the captain in a panic-stricken voice as he shuffled away from the stricken man. "The fellow might be contagious."

Pete's arms shot up above his head, and he tipped his head back. "Booo-hooo-booo!"

The captain stumbled, regained his footing, and said, "What the dickens?"

"Just larking around. It's for my acting repertoire, darling."

The captain's face scrunched into a doughy ball, peanut eyes shrunken to dots. "You are too old to be playing the fool. Explain yourself, man."

Pete extended his chin and moved his jaw from side to side. His eyes closed, mouth opened, and in a voice mimicking Mr Channer said, "Friends, I bring bad news. Tonight's practice is off!"

The captain smashed his cane into the floor. "What the devil are you gibbering about?"

In his normal voice, Pete said, "Ladies and gentlemen, Skegness FM 87.7 just announced in a breaking news section that Mr Channer is a person of interest in the murder investigation of Fiona Fenchurch. The word on the beach is that he was last seen driving out of town, at full speed."

Chapter 32

IT TOOK A MOMENT FOR the words to sink in. Then all at once the lobby filled with shouts.

"Gone where?" cried the stout woman, throwing her arms in the air.

Pete shrugged. "In the opposite direction from here."

Captain Honeybush tapped his cane on the concrete floor. "Order! Ladies and gentlemen, I insist on order!"

Tap-tap-tap.

Tony Pigro, the other security guard, opened his eyes, yawned, and shifted his body weight like a cat about to pounce. In a single movement, which he must have practised, he swung his body into Fred Faul's empty chair. There he settled down, eyes closing.

Unaware of Tony Pigro's seat grab, the short, skinny man with a bald head and protruding eyes said, "What about our pay?"

Again Pete shrugged. "Guess we'll have to chalk up the loss to the lessons-learned column of life."

"Order," bawled the captain, fury blazing in his peanut-brown eyes. "I will have order."

Tap-tap-tap.

The man, dressed as a seagull, flapped his thick feathered wings in frustration. "I was promised an additional fiver an hour for dressing as a bird. Damn hot in here, and it cost a pretty penny to put together too. I want my money!"

Tap-tap-tap.
Tap-tap-tap.
Tap-tap-tap.

"Order, order. I will have order."

It took several more hard whacks of the captain's cane on the floor before the angry shouts of the actors died away.

"Ladies and gentleman," said the captain in a slow superior nasal voice when all was quiet. "Radio reports are notoriously unreliable. You have my word; there is absolutely nothing to worry about. Now, please remain here in the lobby while l call around to establish the facts."

With large military strides, the captain scurried away, his cane smacking against the hard concrete floor like pistol shots in an old, back and white Wild West movie.

Chapter 33

FIFTEEN MINUTES LATER, the captain returned, his face flushed. "It appears Mr Channer... err... has to attend to a... err.. family emergency." The superior nasal authority in his voice seemed diminished and uncertain. "We have your contact details and will be in touch as soon as possible. Dismissed."

Pandemonium broke out.

"What about our money?"

"Is the exhibition cancelled?"

"What about the cost of my bird suit?"

"Dismissed!" yelled the captain as he whacked his cane on the reception desk.

Tony Pigro jerked up. His eyes opened and blinked as if wondering where he was. When at last it came to him, he stood up and saluted the captain. "Ready and willing for duty, sir."

Captain Honeybush turned to the actors, with cane held high in the air, his face purpling, he screamed. "Now, everyone but my security team get the hell out of here before I call the police. The museum will be in contact at the appropriate time."

Reluctant mumbles, grunts, and cursing filled the air as the gaggle of actors shuffled towards the entrance. Captain Honeybush limped at the rear like a shepherd steering his flock. After the last actor left the building, the captain stood for a long moment watching the individuals disperse into the gloom of the car park. With a satisfied grunt, he bolted the door and turned to face his team of security guards—namely Tony Pigro and myself.

"Can't have too many people snooping about the place after dark. We don't want any more discoveries, do we?" The captain pulled out a hip flask and took a long slow gulp. "Tony, old man, why don't you take Fred's seat on reception."

"Righto, sir." Tony eased himself into the chair, leaned back as his feet swung on the desk.

The captain took another long sip from his hip flask and said in a slurred voice, "Mrs Cudlow, Old Gal, please work the archives. You know the way." He paused, placed a hand on his cheek as his blackish tongue darted between his yellowed teeth. "First night alone, eh? Not to worry, I'll stop by a little after midnight to check up on you."

Chapter 34

I MADE MY WAY TO THE *Lincolnshire Weekly* archives reception and bolted the door shut. I was jumpier than a microwave packet of popcorn. Nothing had gone to plan, but at least no one could get into the area unless I unbolted the door.

The heavy musty smell reminded me of a used bookstore. I scrabbled at the light switches hoping this time to find the combination to brighten the room. The ceiling bulbs remained dim.

With the thoroughness of a crime scene technician, I scanned the hazy space.

No cordoned-off area.

No police tape.

Nothing to suggest anything out of the ordinary had occurred only twenty-four hours ago.

And no one hiding in the corners to jump out and scare me.

The room was almost exactly as I found it yesterday. Except only a single I.A. Channer figure stood at the side of the reception desk—the basketball player.

"Thank God they removed the bag lady," I muttered, taking a seat. "Maybe if I have to do this tomorrow night, they'll get rid of you too, Mr Basketball Man."

The figure's dark, shiny eyes seemed to watch me, and I fancied they narrowed a fraction, although I knew that couldn't be true. Still, the thought of it, and that the mannequin might come to life and attack me with those oversized skeleton hands put the hairs up on the back of my neck.

"A trick of the darkness; nothing but a figment of my mental psyche," I said to chase away the unease as I reached into my handbag and pulled out my e-book reader. Tonight, I'd lined up a lighthearted P.G. Woodhouse tale. "Can't beat a fun-filled story with Jeeves to lighten the mood and lift the atmosphere."

After ten minutes of forced effort, I gave up.

On my phone, I pulled up my favourite social media sites. The antics of cats or my Facebook friends didn't hold my attention. I put the phone on the desk and sat and thought about the research I wanted to do on Old Betty.

But I couldn't focus.

After an hour of edgy nothingness, I jumped up, intent on walking around the archives hall. I got as far as placing my hand on the door that led into the main room before my nerve failed. There was nothing in there but shelves filled with files and boxes of old newspapers and yellow clippings, anyway.

Instead, I walked to the basketball player, confirmed again his teeth were Hollywood perfect and eyes were only darkened glass.

"There is no way those orbs narrowed. A physical impossibility," I said with relief. "I guess it is just me, myself, and I in this room tonight."

I heard a movement and felt sure there was someone behind me. I spun around, waving my arms with wild swings through the air before I realised it was the phone vibrating on the desk.

"Doris Cudlow," I said, kicking myself for not checking the screen before I spoke.

"Hullo, hullo, it is Jenny. I called to see how you are getting along. So sorry I couldn't make it this evening, but at my age, well, you'll know how it is one day."

Her voice sounded like a harp played in heaven to my ears. A friendly voice to chase away the shadows in the corners. Another real-life human to share stories, rumours, and gossip.

"Oh, no problem at all. Glad to hear from you." My voice bubbled over with joy. "How are you doing?"

Jenny said, "Fancy joining me for a late afternoon meal at the Fiddlers Bowl Café? They have a back to school special menu at four p.m. this Thursday. My treat for leaving you on your own."

"That sounds delightful," I said. "Thursday at four, it is."

We spoke for an hour about nothing in particular. Then Jenny said, "Everyone's talking about Fiona Fenchurch. The radio station reported someone strangled her. It must have been a person dancing on the beach nearby."

"A man with large hands," I said, easing into the subject as I stared at the thick, spiny skeleton fingers of the I.A. Channer figure. "Like a basketball player."

"But how did the body disappear?" Jenny asked. "I mean, how could a dead body vanish from a crowded beach and end up in the archives? That's impossible."

For a long moment, I let the question swirl around in my brain then I said, "I hear Mr Channer is a person of interest."

Jenny snorted. "Ridiculous! The police are a bunch of buffoons. Mr Channer is an innovative artist not a killer. He has to be, to make a living from his art. "

I considered that carefully and something clicked. "When did Mr Channer stage his first *Bones in the Night, Ghosts in the Day* exhibition?"

"About ten years ago, around the time he'd became fascinated with taxidermy. I remember it as if it were yesterday. His show opened just after the Dancing Hands Mystery. There was a solitary figure in his first exhibition."

I licked my dry lips and said, "Man or woman, do you remember?"

"Oh, let me think... a man... no, a woman. Yes... yes... an older woman, don't recall the details. The following year he added a man, the year after that a mother and child, I believe." Jenny stopped for a moment. When she continued, her voice filled with pride. "Mr Channer's exhibition has become somewhat of a tradition around here. I played a small part in bringing the first event to the museum, and it's been here ever since. The display is immensely popular with the folk who attend the Retirees' Spring Festival. They like to bring their grandchildren to the show against the wishes of their parents. The children don't find it at all scary."

I filtered her words like a prospector panning for gold. Anything obvious that caught my eye, I filed in the back of my mind. At last, as the pieces of the puzzle began to take shape, I said, "What do you think happened to Fiona Fenchurch that day?"

The line fell silent for several moments. "Have you spoken with Constable Wriggly?"

"Briefly. But what the officer said made little sense."

"Nothing about that idle man is intelligible. Maybe you might get a chance to speak with Mr Channer. I believe he was on the beach the day Fiona vanished. Back then he performed in a little show, very talented is Mr Channer. He wore one of those long black Victorian capes."

"On the beach?"

"That's right. It was funeral-director black, went right down to his ankles. I don't know how he wore it in all that heat. The day Fiona disappeared was hotter than today."

"Why would anyone dress in a cape on a sunny beach?"

Jenny grunted. "Why would anyone wheel around a large wooden crate? That's what he did back then, still does it today. I've come to realize artists are a little different from the rest of us." Jenny's voice dropped to a defensive whisper. "Mr Channer and Fiona didn't see eye to eye."

There were a thousand questions I wanted to ask but said, "Do you think Mr Channer was involved in Fiona's death?"

Jenny's voice rose in disgust. "The police are barking up the wrong tree hounding the poor man. Yes, Mr Channer was dancing close to Fiona when she died, he even admits that." Jenny's voice fell silent for a moment, as if she were thinking. Then her voice rose as if alarmed by a disturbing thought. "Perhaps there was a motive. But to kill the poor woman. Goodness knows I won't think any more about it. I simply refuse to believe that of a local artist!"

I said, "Are you sure?"

Jenny's voice took on a wasp like buzz. "Mr Channer might be a miserable sod, but artists don't go around killing people and magicking away their bodies! Now let's put an end to all this nasty gossip about Mr Channer. He is part of our town's cultural fabric, and I will not tolerate idle tittle-tattle. Goodness knows the arts have suffered enough."

After I had let that settle, I said, "Any idea how Fiona's body ended up in an archives storeroom?"

Jenny said, "Now that's the real mystery. The captain manages the inventory, and with the security team, checks the storage rooms regularly. Don't go in there much myself, no need. The one thing we know with certainty is that the body wasn't there a day or so ago. That narrows down the time window and the list of suspects."

I leaned back in my chair and gazed reflectively into the empty space where the bag lady had stood the previous evening. "Right now, it looks as if the police only have Mr Channer in their sights."

"He is a scapegoat for their incompetence. How on earth can they think a man of Mr Channer's artistic leaning would be involved in such butchery?"

"Don't know," I said, thinking the opposite.

"Utter waste of public funds."

"I suppose if he is innocent, the police will figure it out."

"Our county police service is woefully under resourced; they'll never solve it."

There was more than an element of truth in her words. But tonight, of all nights, I wanted to believe justice would eventually be served. Fiona Fenchurch deserved that. I said, "Often something turns up, some small clue that cracks a case wide open."

"Like what?"

"I've no idea."

The sigh from the other end was audible. "Doris, working in the hospice is such an emotional drain, and now someone has dumped Fiona's bones in my sacred archives. It's desecration... enough to make me weep... don't like to point fingers, but the buck should stop at Captain Honeybush."

The line fell silent for several seconds.

When Jenny spoke again, her voice, filled with a mixture of mischief and secrets, regained its usual bubble. "Doris, please don't worry about the captain tonight. I've added a little of my special something to his evening tipple—twice yesterday's dose, and triple in his hip flask!"

Chapter 35

I HUNG UP, PLACED MY phone in my handbag, and sank deep into the reception chair. The conversation with Jenny Styles had eased my anxiety almost as much as Mrs Lintott's famous hot chocolate. A relieved fatigue pressed down on my eyes. My body felt as heavy as if my limbs were filled with Skegness beach sand. I let my eyelids flutter shut.

"Just for a minute. Only a short while to regain my strength."

I fell asleep. Right there at the reception desk to the archives. That was like dozing off in a haunted graveyard at midnight. And it was a deep, dreamless slumber. One that might have lasted until the sun was high in the blue sky.

But a noise woke me up.

A scampering scurrying that wasn't so much a sound as a sensation.

Something brushed against the back of my neck.

My eyes snapped open.

At first, I didn't know where I was. The dimmed ceiling lights saved me from utter confusion, their weak rays cutting through the gloom. The dusty air gradually orientated me back to the present. I sat up, touched the back of my neck and squinted at the clock above the doorjamb—1:45 a.m. I finished at two; the shift was almost over.

A coldness raked along the back of my neck.

Instantly awake, I scrambled to my feet, glanced around, saw no one.

"Don't be silly, Doris. There is nothing to worry about."

A blast of icy air swept over my body.

"What on earth!"

My eyes darted around the room for the source. I'd bolted shut the door to the museum area earlier. The central archives door was closed. There were no windows or air-conditioning vents. A radiator ran along a far wall, but that couldn't possibly be the source.

For what seemed like hours I stood very still waiting, ears strained, eyes focused for even the tiniest of movement.

Nothing.

"Must have come from the... archives room!"

Sweat bloomed in my armpits. I walked to the door of the central archives, blocking out the tiny bubble of fear growing in my stomach. I focused my energy on the door. It took every ounce of willpower for my hand to turn the handle.

The door swung open without a sound.

I stuck my head into the darkness of the archives room, gazed around, saw nothing unusual, and eased the door shut. That was about as far as I was stepping into that room tonight.

"The only reasonable explanation is that it was part of my dream. Little more than a figment of my mental psyche." I spoke the words out loud to ease my fears. To confirm my assertion, I did a slow three hundred and sixty degree turn, eyes raking over every possible source for that frigid blast. It was only when I turned to face the reception desk, I realised something was amiss.

The bag-lady figure stood to one side, the faceless head staring in my direction, feather duster gone.

"What the—"

An icy blast swept over me, sending my nerves into overdrive. For a brief, dreadful second, I saw a flash in the eyes—a long, yellow glow—like the warning beam of a lighthouse at night. A moan sounded close, yet far away as a swirl of mist appeared to engulf the bag lady. I turned, stumbling away from the figure towards the far end of the reception desk, hand outstretched, grasping for my handbag.

It was then I heard a metallic clanking.

Clink-clink-clink.

In a blind panic, I slipped, falling into the basketball player. Its oversized skeleton hands jerked forward clasping tight around my neck. I flung my arms about like a wild beast, striking its melon-sized skull with a fist. Its gigantic head toppled to the ground and shattered into a million fragments. Gravity pulled the headless figure forward. Together we fell, hitting the floor with a soft thud. Entangled in the mannequin's arms, I struggled as we tumbled around wildly. Writhing with every ounce of energy, I screamed, pushed free to my feet and ran.

Chapter 36

I WAS IN THE MAIN LOBBY area with no memory of how I got there. Everything was silent and motionless except for the sound of my shoes which clattered on the concrete floor. Words formed in my dry throat, but no sound came out as I hurried towards the main reception counter.

Tony Pigro, the other overnight security guard, came into view. Thank God.

But he was face down on the desk, a half-empty bottle of rum at his side. The gentle rise and fall of his chest and the soft snore, communicated his had been an uneventful shift.

I didn't stop to wake him.

I kept going, half running, half stumbling, towards the main doors.

At the entrance, I glanced out through the glass pane into the darkened car park. Dizzy with confusion and heart thudding like a sledgehammer, I paused to catch my breath.

A sharp noise almost froze me in place.

Tap-tap-tap.

I hurled myself at the door, grasping the handle and pushing down.

It didn't open.

Tap-tap-tap.

I tugged again, this time pushing with my shoulder.

But it didn't budge.

Tap-tap-tap.

"Mrs Cudlow, Old Gal."

Again, I shoved and suddenly remembered the deadbolt.

Fumbling, I tugged the latch. It moved a fraction. With an almighty heave I pulled.

A metallic click.

It slid.

The door burst open, and I tumbled outside.

Stars twinkled in an inky-black sky. Warm salt air flooded my nostrils. The sound of waves crashing on the shore filled my ears. I hurried down the steps, across the gravel, and with a deft search of my handbag, keys in hand, opened the car door. Only when I was seated inside, the engine started, did I look back towards the Beachside Museum entrance. Silhouetted against the interior light, a figure leaned on a cane.

Chapter 37

AS I DROVE THROUGH the darkened streets of Skegness, I knew there was a logical explanation to what I'd just witnessed, but no matter how often I ran the events through my head, I couldn't make sense of it all.

Then I thought about Fred Faul. His wide eyes were more alert than I'd ever seen as he fled from the museum. His terrified face filled my mind so much I slowed the car.

He'd seen Old Betty... and so had I!

Terror caused me to pull over. I cut the engine and stared out into the quiet street. As I sat there, shaking, I knew if I let fear take over, there'd be no way I'd make it through another night shift, anywhere.

I eased the driver side window open a crack. A blast of warm air poured in, along with the distant roar of the sea crashing against the shore. When I was calm enough to think clearly again, I knew there was only one way to beat this. Finish the article about Old Betty. But I hadn't yet put pen to paper on the first word.

"Got to dig faster into Old Betty, Fiona Fenchurch, and the Dancing Hands Mystery."

I started the engine. A red light on the dashboard flashed. The car was almost out of petrol, again.

"Oh bugger!"

Tonight I wasn't going to take the chance I'd make it home without topping up; not with my nerves rattling louder than a freight train on a rusty track. I pulled out into the main road, turned left into a side street, and eased the old car the short drive towards Skeggy Stop.

There is a sense of elation at the sight of a petrol station familiar to all motorists low on fuel. It was this feeling that washed over me as the bright lights and petrol pumps came into view.

"Going to make it. Things will turn out right side up," I said, pulling up to a pump close to the store entrance.

For several moments I sat still, letting the trembles in my body diminish. What I'd seen, felt, heard, earlier in the reception area to the archives room made little sense. Yet my rational mind wanted to find an explanation. But now wasn't the time for logical thought; now was the time for calm. Sucking in a deep breath, I let the air out gradually.

"One... Two... Three..."

A light tap on the window jolted me out of my controlled breathing.

"Doris Cudlow, isn't it?" A very short, skinny woman with a hooked nose and raven eyes stared through the driver side window. She wore her grey hair in a loose bun, which somehow matched her baggy, sack like dress. It was Mildred, George's wife. "Everything all right, dear?"

With a clammy hand, I wound down the car window. "Almost out of petrol."

"Honey, you look like you've seen a ghost. Come on, get out, and come inside. I've just put on a fresh pot of coffee. George will pump the petrol for you. How much should he put in?"

Coffee sounded good, and I needed to be around humans, alive ones. Right now, even a busybody like Mildred Seeton was better than being alone. "Ten pounds," I said, following her into the store.

George sat behind the counter, sharp nose stuck deep inside a newspaper. Mildred coughed, and they exchanged looks. In an instant, he was on his feet and at the door. "How much?" He held the door open, narrow, squinting eyes staring back and forth between his wife and me.

"Ten," replied Mildred. "No rush."

George's gapped teeth formed a smile as he nodded his head, once again reminding me of a donkey. "Right you are, and I'll give your windows a quick wipe down as well."

Chapter 38

MILDRED BUSTLED TO a wooden counter on which a coffee pot bubbled. She filled two paper cups.

"Milk?"

"Black and strong."

Mildred's quick eyes flashed a birdlike glance. "That bad, eh?" She added milk and sugar to her cup, stirred with a swizzle stick and said, "So, Mrs Cudlow, what is going on?"

To say I felt something cold on my arm, heard noises, saw something swirly, and ran, sounded silly, especially for a security guard. "Fine. I'm fine."

"You sure?"

I didn't know. But there was one thing I'd learned about English seaside towns—gossip and rumours ebbed and flowed as regularly as the daily tide. First, it's Mildred who tells Mrs McLaughlin, who tells her husband, Jack, who mentions something at the model railway club to Pete Brown, who shares it with his wife. Pretty soon the whole town knows, and you are at the centre of everyone's gossip. I didn't want that.

I said, "All is good, now."

"Honey, you sound a little shook up. What happened?"

"Nothing I can talk about."

"Now, now. Let's not be playing silly buggers. Honey, I'm listening?"

When I didn't answer immediately, Mildred's eyes narrowed. "Oh, I see, you think I'm a busybody, do you?"

"Oh no!"

"Then take a sip of that coffee, and tell old Mildred all about it." She stared, her raven-dark eyes bright and very eager. "I hear you covered a shift for Grace Rivers yesterday. George told me all about it, like it was a big clandestine operation. It was somewhat disappointing to hear it from my husband rather than the horse's mouth. We women have to stick together... and share."

I took a sip. It tasted more of the cup than the actual coffee. "Oh, I didn't mean to keep it a secret."

"Good, then it is not going to hurt anyone to tell me what happened tonight, is it?"

"It is something I'm still processing."

Mildred pursed her lips. "I get it. You want to tell Mrs Lintott first, eh? Well, we two are like sisters, and I'm older than her, so come on, spit it out."

"It's been a trying few days. I'm sure you understand."

Mildred gave a faint smile like a gold miner uncovering the first nugget. "Can't imagine finding a real body, especially one that is all... dried bones, and in that place."

We both knew "that place" referred to the Beachside Museum.

"Not a night I want to relive," I said, my voice raspy.

"And what about tonight? You look like something dreadful happened." Mildred's eyes widened, and she licked her lips. "Another skeleton?"

"Goodness, no!"

Disappointment flashed in her dark eyes. "Something else, then?"

If I told her about the rattling chains and spooky swirls, she'd think I was a little tipsy, and that would make her gossip even more delicious to share. Best to forget about it for now, I told myself. But for that to happen I needed to find a replacement in case Joey was still sick. The thought of working another overnight shift at the Beachside Museum was impossible, right now. I said, "They are a little short on security guards at the museum. Do you know anyone who'd like a job?"

Mildred shuddered. "You'd never get me working an overnight shift in that place."

"Not for the faint hearted," I said, still hoping she'd offer up a name or two. "But they pay well, and most nights, they say, there is little to do. Good for a retired person, or someone who wants to pick up a night shift."

Mildred shook her head. "Can't say I know of anyone ...the rumours, you see. Not too many locals want to work there, apart from the odd drunk. You're from out of town, so I suppose it's different."

"Well, if you think of a name or two—"

Mildred swirled her coffee. "Fred Faul was in here earlier, as pale as a porcelain doll. He claimed to have heard spooky noises and saw a ghost. But the man is always half-drunk, so I took it with a pinch of salt. That was until..." Her eyes drifted off in the direction of the Beachside Museum.

"Until..." I said, in the way of encouragement and hoping it would give her time to think of a name or two, drunk or not.

"Oh, I don't like to gossip." Mildred gestured with her paper cup to the chilled beer on the far wall. "They say the overnight security guards at the Beachside Museum spend their time drinking and playing cards. Can't be true, can it?"

"Not my experience," I said, then remembered Tony Pigro. "But I'm not much of a gambler. Don't drink much, either."

"Oh dear, I'm not talking about you. It's the likes of Fred Faul who booze on the job. "

"I see."

Mildred's eyes sharpened. "The thing is Fred is not the sort to leave an easy job without putting up a hell of a fight."

I said, "He's made a career out of security work."

"Never in a bank, though. Always some place comfortable where he can booze and snooze."

"I wouldn't like to say."

Mildred ignored my comment. "Fred said he'll never go back, not even to visit during the day. That's how I know it wasn't the booze talking." Her chin jutted towards the Beachside Museum. "Something really happened tonight. You worked Grace's shift; did you see anything?"

"Mr Channer's exhibits made me a little shaky, that's all." Silently I prayed Joey was bouncing around in his bed and demanding to go back to school to play with his friends. Failing that I half wondered if sitting in a spooky room was something Mrs Lintott might quite enjoy.

Mildred touched her cheek. "Can't blame you. The grandchildren seem to like it, though. I don't know why, too many statues of children for my taste. Enough children go missing around these parts without having them on display in an exhibition. The police don't do much about it, though." There was a pause. Then she spoke in a cryptic voice. "Not that I'm one to spread gossip, but they say she was his first victim, and now it is payback time."

Whether it was because part of my mind was still processing what had happened earlier or that I wasn't great with riddles, I said, "Sorry, Mildred, I'm not following you."

Mildred took a birdlike sip from her cup. "Fiona Fenchurch disappeared ten years ago. About the same time as Mr Channer's gruesome show began. The word on the beach is she was his first exhibit."

Chapter 39

THE STORE DOOR OPENED and closed. It barely registered, so focused was I on Mildred. I took a sip of coffee. "When you say the first exhibit, you don't mean—"

"In his *Bones in the Night, Ghosts in the Day* exhibition," said Mildred. "Everyone is talking about it. Please don't think I'm spreading rumours, but they say Mr Channer did away with Fiona and put her body on display as part of his gruesome art."

"Exactly," said Constable Wriggly. I hadn't noticed when he entered the store. "Mr Channer is a definite person of interest."

Mildred's eyes twinkled. "That's what Skegness FM 87.7 reported. What else can you tell us, Officer?"

Constable Wriggly's voice took on a formal tone. "Nothing, because we have an ongoing investigation underway. I just popped in for a couple of those microwavable sausage rolls. I find they are passable cold. Do you have any in stock?"

Mildred's eyes narrowed as if she were performing a mental calculation. "How about I warm them up?"

"That'll be lovely."

She hurried to the refrigerator, pulled out two packets which she placed in a microwave oven. Forty-five seconds later Constable Wriggly held the zapped pastries on a paper plate.

"Ummm, ummm, delicious!" He shoved an entire sausage roll into his mouth and chewed vigorously. "Excellent pastries. Nothing like 'em when hunger strikes."

"You were telling us about the Dancing Hands Mystery," Mildred said, her canny eyes watching the officer as he ate.

"Was I? Oh yes! I told Inspector Doxon I remembered seeing Mr Channer on the beach, very close to the body the day Fiona disappeared." Constable Wriggly licked his fingers and picked up the second sausage roll. "Captain Honeybush helped guard the body. I re-read his original official statement last night during a quiet moment on duty."

"What did it say?" Mildred spoke fast as if her access to the information diminished with every bite.

Constable Wriggly nibbled the edge of the second pastry. "The captain saw Mr Channer hovering about the victim. That's the relevant part, not sure how I missed it the first time around. I guess I'm more seasoned now, almost a detective, really."

Mildred nodded. "One wonders how the detective rank has eluded you all these years."

Constable Wriggly rubbed his chin. "The Dancing Hands Mystery doomed my chances. Judge Eboch presided over the investigation. He almost threw me out of the police force. That case has haunted me for a decade. Now we have a body, and soon enough, the killer will be behind bars. This one is personal; I'll do everything in my power to crack this case." He popped the rest of the pastry into his mouth and munched.

Mildred let out a thwarted sigh then threw out a desperate last question. "Is it true Mr Channer has left town?"

The constable's voice returned to its formal tone. "A criminal can run from the Lincolnshire Police Force, but they can't hide for long. He'll be found, and when he is, I want to be the officer to book him."

Chapter 40

I THREW THE GEAR STICK into neutral, flipped off the ignition, stared out of the window, and quietly let out a long sigh.

Two forty-five a.m.

Home.

Safe.

The street was empty. Mrs Lintott's kitchen window was bathed in darkness, and nothing moved in the still night air. I leaned forward on the steering wheel and thought back to my experiences in the museum. A cold sweat broke out on my forehead as my mind filled with a jumble of images and sounds—the basketball player, the bag lady, the metallic rattling, and the swirl of mist. In all of that did I also hear a voice?

With a mind oddly clarified by lack of sleep and fear, I stared through the windscreen into the darkened street. Yes, there was a voice! It sounded close yet far away, pitiful, like the agonised cried of a wounded beast, but it was definitely a female voice. It might have been of a little girl or a grown woman; I couldn't tell. The anguish in the moan masked the age.

"Safer to walk alone in the nightclub district at midnight on a Friday night than the Beachside Museum."

Of course, I admitted to myself, one did occasionally read of trouble outside of the nightclubs in the town centre. Hadn't Constable Wriggly complained about a raucous gang of pensioners getting into a fight over who won the 1987 English Football Association Cup final? Still, you couldn't say it was common.

"Don't be silly, Doris. There is a rational explanation, and the Beachside Museum is way safer than the midnight streets of the nightclub district."

The words encouraged my spirits. It was time, I decided, to start researching in earnest into Old Betty. Whether I could sell the article to a local newspaper no longer mattered. I was curious.

I climbed out of the car, legs still a little shaky, locked the door, and took a step or two.

Something moved in the shadows.

Clink-clink-clink.

There wasn't time to think, only react. My legs did that for me. With giant steps, they hurried up the stairs of Whispering Towers Boarding House, only turning around once I had the front door open.

A plump cat crept low to the ground, collar tinkering as it moved.

"Too jumpy!" I muttered. "Just one of Mr Felix's cat friends. Way too jumpy, Doris."

Chapter 41

LATER, SITTING ON MY bed, after having had a shower and dipped into a novel, my heart still pounded, and my mind raced. I couldn't settle.

"That petrol station coffee has a wild kick!"

Then it struck me.

I needed a drink, an alcoholic drink.

As I tried to concentrate on something other than the cans of beer in the fridge, I slowly rose to my feet and slinked on the tips of my toes to the kitchen. All at once, the urge was overwhelming. Like a starving man brought a three-course meal, I threw open the refrigerator door and grasped the six-pack in my shaking hand.

Tearing off a can, I muttered, "Just one, and a sleeping pill. That ought to do it."

I raised the cold can to eye level to read the label:

Refresh your body and mind with a hoppy, malty, local brew.

"Just what I need."

With the can in hand, I tiptoed to the bathroom.

Thud, thud, thud.

"Sorry, Mr Pandy, need medicinal help to wash away the memories from the day."

For a moment, I stared at my reflection in the tiny mirror on the medicine cabinet door.

"Who are you kidding? Doris, you can't pretend anymore. You're a drunk and drug addict—get used to it."

I yanked open the door feeling hopeless. After a frantic moment, I found the tiny brown bottle I was looking for. It was half full.

"Good. I'll take two."

The telephone rang as the cabinet door snapped shut. I jerked in surprise. Who would call at such a late hour?

I could think of only one person—Toby. And the news had to be bad.

I stood there for a few moments in a state of frozen shock. Then with care not to disturb Mr Pandy, but with quick steps, I found my way to the kitchen. Placing the pills and the can of beer on the table, I picked up the phone, my mind braced for the worst.

"Hello," I said without glancing at the screen. "Doris Cudlow here."

"Thank you. Thank you!" It was Grace Rivers. "Knew you'd be coming home from the shift about now. You're not in bed, yet, are you?"

"Not yet, no. But it has been one hell—"

"It's Joey!"

I pressed the phone to my ear. "What's happened?"

"His temperature has broken. The kid's sitting up in bed asking for ice cream. Can you believe it?"

I felt light headed as she spoke, knowing I wouldn't have to work another shift at the Beachside Museum. "That is wonderful news. I'm not sure about the ice cream, though."

Grace laughed. "Me neither. I told him he must wait until next weekend. How did the shift go?"

"That's what I wanted to speak with you about. The shift was—"

A child's voice called in the background.

"Sorry, Doris, I've got to go, just wanted to thank you for helping me out. I'll be able to pick up my shifts from now on, and even better news, Fred Faul's quit, so I'll take his. Lord knows I need the money. See you at the opening of the I.A. Channer exhibition tomorrow night. It starts at seven."

Grace hung up.

Placing the phone back on the table, I leaned back in the chair, letting a feeling of warmth wash over me. I'd helped Grace out, covered her back, even though I felt like giving up. Even though I'd wanted to run away. For the first time in a long while, I felt a sense of accomplishment.

After a moment, I got to my feet, beer can in one hand and the pill bottle in the other.

"I'll warn Grace about Old Betty after I've had a nap and my mind is clearer."

At the fridge, I opened the door and placed the can inside. In the tiny bathroom, I did the same with the pill bottle.

"Yes, I'm an alcoholic, but that doesn't mean I have to drink."

Chapter 42

THE NEXT DAY A SOFT knock woke me from a deep sleep. I sat up groggily, trying to figure out whether I was still in a dream or reality. It was a combination of pain shooting along my back, a dull throb in my temples, and someone still pounding on the door that confirmed I was no longer in the blissful land of Nod.

"Yoo hoo, Doris, are you up?"

"I am now," I grumbled.

Ignoring my grouch, Mrs Lintott bustled into the room, carrying a tray. Mr Felix trotted at her side. She placed it on the kitchen table then hurried to the curtains, swept them aside, and opened the windowpane.

"What time is it?" The bedsit clock only required a slight turn of my head, but I was too tired for that much movement this early in the day.

"Almost three p.m." Mrs Lintott pointed to the tray on my kitchen table. "I've brought you an afternoon breakfast."

The smell of the fried bacon, scrambled eggs, baked beans, mushrooms, and black pudding had me sliding out of bed.

"Brought a pot of fresh coffee too," added Mrs Lintott. "Let me pour you a cup, and you can dig in."

There is something unladylike about clambering out of bed to stuff one's face with beans, bacon, eggs, and fried pigs' blood. But I'd grown so used to Mrs Lintott, that I no longer pretended to be other than who I was. And right now that was a woman hungry for breakfast and coffee.

As I slurped and munched, Mrs Lintott let out a little chuckle. Her voice tinkled as if there was something she was eager to share. "Take your time, love, else you'll get hiccups."

"Ummm, okay... Ummm, thank you."

The caffeine hadn't yet hit my bloodstream as Mrs Lintott explained the purpose of her visit.

"Oooh, Doris, the telephone's been ringing all day. I've hardly had a moment's peace. That's why I've come up here."

"Ummm... what's.... ummm... going on?"

"It's my bingo ladies. They are all in a lather, and it's my fault."

I took a quick gulp of coffee and smiled as the caffeine began to do its job. "What's got your friends so upset?"

Mrs Lintott tugged at her ear. "You!"

"Eh?" I drained the mug and refilled. But Mrs Lintott's words had me wide awake. "Me?"

With a slow, deliberate movement, Mrs Lintott nodded. "I told everyone the bet with the postie was a dead certainty. How was I to know you'd smash up one of the exhibits last night?"

The caffeine kicked in. It all came back—Old Betty, the rattling chains, and the basketball player. I said in a high-pitched squeal, "The bag lady appeared, and the basketball player with monster hands toppled forward and grasped at my throat. And there was a swirl of..." My voice trailed off as I realised how ridiculous the whole thing sounded.

"Love, what are you going on about?"

No matter how much I explained what happened, it wouldn't make any sense. So I said, "Mrs Lintott, have you any idea how dark it is in that museum? It's a wonder people aren't bumping into things every day."

Mrs Lintott tutted. "That postie is craftier than a fox. Why, he didn't even mention the lighting situation when he took our money. I ought to—"

"Now, now, Mrs Lintott," I said, thinking fast. "Maybe there is a lesson in all of this."

"Like what?"

"Err... don't... gamble."

"Don't be silly. Having a little flutter is part of Skegness life. Where would the fun be if we couldn't make a bet here and there? It'd be like living in one of those Carmelite convents where talk is banned. Imagine it, Doris, only the sounds of prayers and mouths chomping over dinner!"

I took a bite of toast and chewed. "Ummm... err... doesn't bear thinking about."

Mrs Lintott wrung her hands. "Oooh, Doris, how am I going to live this one down with my bingo ladies?"

I chewed and thought. "A man like the postie is always taking bets. All you have to do is bide your time and wait."

Mrs Lintott sighed. "One of these days we'll wipe 'em out."

I blew on the surface of the coffee. "As long as I'm not the centre of the bet, I'm with you on that. Thank you for breakfast."

She waved her hand in a frustrated gesture. "Oh, that's not why I came up here."

"No?"

A strong breeze ruffled the curtains at the bedsit window. I poured another cup of coffee and nibbled on the edge of a slice of toast all the while waiting for Mrs Lintott to continue.

"Oooh, Doris, I can't get the woman out of my mind."

"Who?"

"Fiona Fenchurch." Mrs Lintott spoke the words in a slow, sober tone, but her lips trembled with a rumour-monger's pleasure.

"Did you know her?"

"No... but I didn't need to. It must have been awful. Can you imagine it, love? Murdered on a beach while everyone about danced, including the killer, and as if that wasn't wicked enough, your body is put on display as part of an art exhibition—and by the very same person who did you in. Oooh, it doesn't bear thinking about."

"Fiona's body wasn't exactly on display. It was hidden in a storeroom!"

"Let's not argue over the details. Her body was found at the museum, and that's where they display things." Now Mrs Lintott's voice squealed with the delight of a squirrel discovering a hoard of its neighbour's nuts. "Oooh, Doris, I wish that were an end to it. A little bird tells me they stored Mr Channer's first exhibit in the *Lincolnshire Weekly* archives. In a room at the back, love."

I spread my hands, palms down, on the table, and for a moment or so I was completely wrapped up in my thoughts. Then I said, "That must be the room where I found the body!"

Mrs Lintott nodded. "That's what Constable Wriggly figured. By all accounts, the storerooms are like kitchen drawers. They throw things in all higgledy-piggledy."

I said, "Now it all makes sense, but it is scarcely believable."

The excited squirrel chirp in Mrs Lintott's voice rose an octave. "Oh, love, it is terrible. The streets of Skegness aren't safe. They say Constable Wriggly is like a man possessed over this case. He's even working longer hours, so he can track down Mr Channer and make the arrest. He's become like one of those television detectives, all narrowed eyed and sharp faced. Never thought I'd see the day."

"This is Skegness, not some massive, anonymous city," I said. "I guess people will be hiding in their homes until Mr Channer is caught."

"Oooh, Doris, it's atrocious! The depravity of mankind knows no bounds. Me and the bingo ladies are going to the opening of the exhibition on Tuesday evening. Are you coming?"

"Do you think it will go ahead?"

"Oh yes, love. It's a sell-out crowd. The whole town will be there. Who knows how many bodies that evil man has on display? We are taking Nurse Phillips with us. She will be our eyes and ears; not that we expect to find anything, but you never know, do you, love?"

Chapter 43

THE SUN WAS LOW IN the sky, and a light mist had rolled in from the sea when we pulled into the Beachside Museum car park that Tuesday evening. Constable Wriggly, all narrowed eyed and sharp faced, waved us into a tight space at the side of the building. I tapped the steering wheel with my fingers, anxiously staring out at the gathering crowd, biting my bottom lip.

"Oooh, it's so exciting," said Mrs Lintott. "Look, even Doctor Bellamy's showed up." A stooped, grey-haired figure in a three-piece suit hurried towards the entrance. A plump woman in a white summer dress struggled to keep pace at his side. "And he's with Nurse Phillips."

"That's Nurse Phillips?" I'd seen her somewhere before. It took a moment, then I said, "Yes, she was on the beach the other day, but she wore a blue nurse's uniform."

"Oh yes, she has a little side hustle helping out at the retirement community homes," said Mrs Lintott as she hurried to unbuckle her seat belt.

A mass of people swirled towards the main doors. It seemed as if the whole town had turned out for the opening of the *Bones in the Night, Ghosts in the Day* exhibition.

Mrs Lintott pushed open the car door. "Come on, Doris, or we'll miss the action."

I said, "Okay, I'll meet you inside."

"Right you are, love," she said, running ahead. "I'll get a ride home with Mrs McLaughlin."

I stared through the car window as Mrs Lintott disappeared into the throng then took a moment to calm my mind, get myself together before going back inside the museum. As I thought over what I'd experienced the other night, I became persuaded to turn around and go home. And I would have to, if it wasn't for Grace Rivers. I knew she was back at work, and I wanted to catch up with her, find out about Joey, and warn her about the ghost of Old Betty.

With hesitation, but resolute, I climbed out of the car. There was a gentle breeze, and I could hear the waves crashing on the beach rustling and mixing with the murmur of the crowd. For a while I stood watching the swirls of excited people hurry across the car park. George and Mildred, the couple who ran the Skeggy Stop petrol station, raced towards the entrance. The postie stood just outside the main door, notepad in hand, weasel face half tilted skyward as if in great thought. Then I took in a deep breath of the salty sea air and joined the masses.

Chapter 44

IT WAS A STREET MARKET inside.

Hundreds of people crowded into the cool lobby area. They swarmed out of the gift shop, along the staircases, and around the reception desk. Pensioners, children, mothers with babies, and people in wheelchairs, waiting in crooked lines by lobby elevators.

A hand touched my back.

"Doris, wonderful to see you."

I half glanced over my shoulder to see Jenny Style's beaming face, reading glasses perched at the end of her nose.

"Wow! It is so busy," I said, smiling back.

"Crazy mad, but amazing!" Jenny threw her hands in the air. Then she danced. "The museum's seen nothing like it since I've been here, and that's years. I suppose Mr Channer's exhibition is like a snowball. Every year it gets a little bigger until it becomes an avalanche. We've only got one police officer to help manage things, Constable Wriggly. We might have to up the number next year." She stopped abruptly, her eyes staring towards the gift shop.

I followed her gaze. At the entrance, dressed in an orange-and-pink, flowing gown, stood a scrawny woman with sharp eyes. I recognised her instantly—the woman I'd seen dancing on the beach in a skimpy bikini. But I couldn't recall her name.

"I keep seeing that woman. Do you know her name?"

Jenny glanced at me sideways through her reading glasses. "Probably in town for the Retirees' Spring Festival, attracts all sorts. I'd better get back to the archives. See you later."

I watched Jenny stride quickly into the crowd.

"Doris!" The cry came from a pale face with bright red lips in a hooded cloak. Pete Brown dodged through the crowd. On his head, an extraordinary long top hat tottered. It was like the one I'd seen on Mr Channer's head, only with a dozen tiny candles that formed a bird's nest.

"Damn busy in here," Pete said, dabbing at his forehead. "Scaring people isn't so easy when the crowd is this large."

"Think of the pay," I said, half wishing I'd taken the acting job. "Is the museum paying you extra, for the crush?"

"I wish, but no." He wobbled his head from side to side. The candles flashed. "Like the hat? Got it on eBay. Only ten quid. The little kids love it, think I'm a magician. And it's better than carrying around that damn scythe. It kept hitting the exhibits, and I don't want them deducting the cost of any damage from my pay." Pete turned and waved.

I followed his gaze.

The woman in the orange-and-pink, flowing gown waved back.

I said, "Who is that woman?"

"Emily Johnson." He stopped speaking as if that was all I needed to know.

"But who is she?" I persisted. "I mean I saw her dancing on the beach the other day, in next to nothing."

Pete let out a chuckle. "That sounds like Emily. Don't see her much these days, but she is looking good. She left Skegness about ten years ago to live in a hippy commune in Wales. I guess she is back now." Pete paused for a moment as if in great thought. "Emily worked as the Skegness Grammar School head librarian. I hear she is back in her old job. If you want to know anything about this area or the historical figures who once lived here, she is your person. Anyway, I've got to find myself a little hidey-hole."

"To jump out and scare people?"

"No, to recharge. These crowds are draining on my creative juices. I'm gonna find a nice quiet corner where I can get forty winks. Then it'll be showtime. See you later."

Pete vanished into the crowd even faster than Jenny.

Chapter 45

AS THE CROWD CONTINUED to grow I thought about Grace Rivers. I wanted to tell her about Old Betty and discover how Joey was getting along.

"Doubt she'll have much time for a chat given the size of this crowd."

I turned towards the reception desk. A woman security guard sat behind the counter as stiff as a board with a large gaggle of people about her. Even from this distance, I could tell it wasn't Grace.

As I made my way through the crowd, I got a better look. The woman wore a crisp dark uniform and the simple cream blouse I'd seen in the storeroom. A hat balanced at a precarious angle on top of a mop of black, frizzy hair from under which a long plait curled along her left cheek. Her skin was smooth, dark brown, and her wide eyes reflected a combination of terror and panic.

"Tim wants the toilet; where are they?" barked a stooped lady in a blue T-shirt. A child, not over seven, clung on to her hand.

"Can I use this voucher to buy sweets from the gift shop?" The question came from a weedy, undersized teenage girl with a round head atop a pale, swanlike neck.

A short, round man with a fringe of grey hair poking out from under a cloth cap yelled, "Where are the real-life bodies? I came here from East Kirkby to see the bodies!" He jabbed a spidery finger at the security guard.

The security guard's eyes darted about like a bird wary of a predator. Sweat trickled down the sides of her cheeks. Frazzled, was an understatement. I knew how she felt, so I tried to help out. "The toilets are right here in the lobby," I said to the stooped lady woman in the blue T-shirt. Then I turned to the weedy teenager. "Yes, those vouchers are good in the shop." Finally, to the man in the cloth hat, I said, "Go up one flight of stairs, and keep your eyes peeled."

"Thank you," said the woman security guard in a trembling voice. Beads of sweat glistened on her forehead. "Today has been one crazy mess."

"Doris Cudlow," I said, extending a hand to make her feel more at ease. "I've worked a shift or two here. Are you new?"

"Alicia Osborn. I started today. Captain Honeybush said the museum would be quiet." She pulled out a handkerchief and dabbed her moist brow. "Not right now, though, with all the news about I.A. Channer on the run and the unanswered questions surrounding the Dancing Hands Mystery."

"It is not normally like this," I said to ease her nerves. "Have you worked as a security guard before?"

"No. Not sure if this is for me, but I've been out of work for so long I'll give just about anything a try. That's what I told Captain Honeybush, and he gave me the job, on a trial basis. Right now it is tough to find a position in Skegness; there are no vacancies." Her voice rose to a shrill. "Nothing, not even a job in a coffee shop wiping tables!"

"I hear you."

Alicia's voice took on a defeated tone. "Got a degree in English. Can't do much with that except teach, I suppose, and right now I can't even get a job doing that."

"I understand where you are coming from. We all need to make a little money to pay the bills. I'm sure you'll have a fun time here."

Alicia wrinkled her nose. "The captain is rather... grabby." Her voice dropped, and she changed the subject. "I've got to give a personal tour to a group of dignitaries from the town of Anderby later, friends of the captain. Mrs Jackson, the chairperson of the museum board, will be attending. I'm not looking forward to that. Maybe I should go to grad school?"

I let out a sympathetic murmur. Part of me wanted to mention journalism, but I didn't want to send her along the same dead-end route that haunted my life. "Maybe a master's degree in accountancy?"

We both laughed.

I said, "Alicia. Do you know Grace Rivers?"

Her gaze dropped to the counter. "Yes, I've heard the name... from Captain Honeybush."

That cheered my spirits. She would know the whereabouts of Grace, and that would spare my sore feet the pain of walking from room to room. I said, "Do you know where she is stationed tonight? I'd like to touch base with her."

Alicia tugged at the lock of hair on her left cheek. "Grace was fired. Captain Honeybush sent her home earlier today."

Chapter 46

"IT DOESN'T MAKE ANY damn sense! Why would the captain fire Grace on such a busy day?" A headache formed at my temples.

Alicia shrugged and avoided eye contact. "Guess you'll have to ask Grace... or Captain Honeybush."

As the headache formed I was torn between asking Alicia more questions and calling Grace. Speak with Alicia first, I told myself, then chat with Grace to fill in the details.

I was about to ask a follow-up question when a tall no-nonsense-type woman, in a business suit, with reddish-black hair pulled into a chic twisted knot said in a superior tone, "I'm Mrs Jackson and have a party with me from Anderby, and I'm told by Captain Honeybush that you will give our group a personal tour of the museum."

Alicia half curtsied, half bowed. "Yes, madame. I'd be delighted to accompany your distinguished group around our splendid premises."

I stepped away from the reception counter. Alicia's hands would be full, so I decided to call Grace. I found a quiet alcove at the far end of the lobby. It was a small hidey-hole that appeared to have once held a coin-operated payphone.

Grace answered on the first ring.

I put on my best New York accent and said, "What's going on, girlfriend?"

"Doris?"

"Who else were you expecting?"

"Nobody."

But I knew from the tone of her voice that wasn't true. "Is everything all right?"

"Going well. Very well—"

"Don't give me that. I'm at the Beachside Museum. What happened?"

Grace's voice broke into bitter sobs. "Can't talk about it."

Journalists are taught it is often better to come at a difficult topic sideways. People often talk when you lighten up the atmosphere. I tried that now. "How is Joey?"

There was a long gasping sob, difficult to tell whether from joy or otherwise. But what Grace said next caused me to suck in a sharp, desperate breath.

"The poor boy took a turn for the worse when I got home."

I breathed out slowly then said, "But he was asking for ice cream."

"I know... I know... but he's relapsed."

"Has Doctor Bellamy been back out to see him?"

"No, he has the day off, but the stand-in doctor visited. He prescribed a new course of pills. If there is no improvement in the next day or so they will admit him to hospital."

Hospitals weren't a place I enjoyed, not even visiting. Too many memories of loved ones going in alive, and coming out cold in a grey box. "Call me if that happens. I'll come in with you."

"On no, Doris, I couldn't possibly impose on you like that."

"If you don't call me, I'll never speak to you again."

The line went silent for a long time.

When Grace spoke, her voice was as soft and low as the flutter of butterfly wings. "Thank you."

I said, "Now are you going to tell me why you got fired?"

"So you know about it, then?"

"Of course. I spoke with the new security guard, Alicia Osborn."

"It wasn't my fault."

"What happened?"

The line went silent for several seconds. Then came a long, low whistle of air, like a cooktop kettle on the boil.

"It was Captain Honeybush."

I said, "What about the odious, little man?"

"He got creepy. So I kicked him... hard in the shins."

Chapter 47

IF THERE WAS ONE THING I knew about Grace Rivers, it was that she knew how to defend herself. And it seemed she'd given the captain what he deserved. But there was only one problem, and it was a big one.

Grace said, "Now I'm out of work. You know what the situation is here in town. How am I going to pay my bills?" The sobs returned. "Maybe I should have just let him—"

"No, girl, you did the right thing."

"Doris, you don't understand."

"Then fill me in."

"There were witnesses."

"Good for you, girl."

"No not to Captain Honeybush being creepy."

"Then to what?"

"Me kicking him. I may have added a punch or two."

I said, "Nothing more than he deserved, I'm sure."

Grace's voice filled with regret. "I've made such a mess of my life and everything else. I was hoping the captain might call so I could apologise. Do you think I should pop around to see him in person after the museum opens tomorrow?"

When you are down in the gutter you need people who can pull you up and help you do the right thing. I played that role now for Grace and dialled my voice to motivational-speaker optimism on steroids. "Never! Stand your ground, girl. You are a princess warrior—lance the boil." Then I added with even more enthusiasm. "Even in Skegness, there are other jobs just waiting to be filled."

"You know," said Grace in a low voice, "I'm one pay cheque away from living on the streets. Without this job"—her voice trailed off into a sob—"me and Joey are destitute."

That struck close to home, and I knew it was true. Pulling deep from the lessons learned in my acting class I said, "Then... the only way is up from here." My voice rose to a triumphant squeal. "Shoot for the moon. If you miss, you'll hit the stars."

After a moment Grace spoke in an upbeat tone. "Yes, you are right. I've ditched one nasty job. I'm sure with your help I can find something much better."

"With more money and right here in town," I added, joining the bandwagon of positivity.

"And better hours." Grace's voice chirped like a songbird.

Enjoying a sense of elation, I said, "The streets of Skegness are overflowing with hidden job opportunities." Then I added, with the extreme exaggeration of a tabloid journalist, "Hundreds of vacancies, right here in town. Grace, you'll never have to work for the likes of Captain Honeybush again. You will find a job of your dreams. I guarantee it."

"Are you sure?"

"Without a shadow of a doubt," I said with the certainty of a politician up for election. "You've got it, girl!"

Another sob by Grace, this time, filled with joy. "Thank you for being such a wonderful, uplifting friend."

"That's what friends are for. Is there anything I can help you with right now?"

"Yes, point me in the direction of all those hidden local vacancies you mentioned. I'll apply right away."

My voice wavered. "I'll have to"—now wasn't the time to mention my own failed job search, and my mind turned over, fast—"do a little digging."

Grace, all eager, said, "Wonderful. Can I ask another favour?"

"Of course."

"I left my cassette recorder at the museum. Can you pick it up for me?"

"Sure. Where did you leave it?"

"In the reception desk drawer in the lobby area—"

"Got it," I said, interrupting. "Girl, I am on this."

"Of the *Lincolnshire Weekly News* archives section."

"Eh?" A cold shiver ran along my spine, but I kept my voice upbeat, although my words came out slow. "Did you say the *Lincolnshire Weekly News* archives reception room?"

"That's right. I pressed record when the captain came into the archives area. It might have captured him being creepy. I left in such a hurry I clean forgot it. It is in the drawer on the side where the I.A. Channer basketball player stood."

"I see. In the reception desk drawer?"

"That's right. Thanks for picking it up for me." Grace let out a long sigh then said, "You never told me how you ended up smashing the I.A. Channer figure into a thousand pieces. Anyway, they've taken it away for repair. Can't say I was too disappointed at that. Oh, and could you put in a word for me at your doughnut-frying place? Fantasy Gardens, isn't it?"

"You don't want to work there," I said, deep in thought about returning to the archives area.

"Why not?"

"You are too good for that. Girl, you are a warrior princess."

"Without any money, job, or knight in shining armour."

I said, "That's true." For a moment I tried to think of something to say, gave up, and repeated myself in an upbeat tone. "That is very true."

"It will be fun frying doughnuts together, don't you think?"

"Of course." But I didn't want to tell her the place was shuttered. "It's cramped and hot; you sure you wouldn't rather go for something else?"

"I need a job. I'll take anything. Will you put in a good word for me?"

After a long barren moment, I said, "It closed down."

Grace spoke fast, as if she'd placed a hand on a hot pipe. "Where are you working now?"

I hesitated, not wanting to speak. "In between jobs, but I'm optimistic." It was supposed to sound positive, but came out with a strong whiff of desperation.

"Oh." Only a single word from Grace, but its tone and the way it was drawn out, signalled the end of our motivational session. We fell into silence for what seem like several minutes but was only a matter of seconds. At last, in a disheartened voice, Grace said, "Do you know the captain is part of the old boys' network and good friends with Judge Eboch?"

"So I've heard." I also knew the judge was renowned for ordering massive fines and long stints in prison, but I didn't mention that.

Grace's voice cracked, and through tearful sobs she said, "The captain is pressing charges."

"Nothing to worry about, girl." I forced the words to take on a positive lilt. "At most you'll get a slap on the wrist."

Grace's voice fell to the lifeless tone of a funeral director. "Captain Honeybush told the police to throw the book at me. Constable Celia Bell has already visited to take a statement."

"Well, the police have to go through their procedure. Just a formality, I'm sure." I tried to maintain the optimism, but the words came out as defeated as a fallen lemon soufflé.

"The case will come before Judge Eboch—common assault and battery."

"Oh bugger!"

Chapter 48

AFTER I HUNG UP AND dropped the phone in my handbag, I stood in that little booth in a quiet corner of the main lobby, staring out at the surge of humanity and wiping the dried tears off my face. Tears for Grace, for her son, and for the other women who'd suffer at the hands of Captain Honeybush.

But what could I do?

"Nothing," I muttered with a bitter breath. "Men like the captain destroy anything that gets in their way." The evil toad was on his way to crushing Grace, and there was absolutely nothing I could do about it.

"The old boys' network is an impenetrable shield."

Fears about returning to the Lincolnshire archives room to retrieve Grace's cassette recorder intensified my defeated mood. Crazy thoughts of spooks and phantoms fanned flames of dread that deepened my feeling of doom.

I didn't want to visit the archives area.

Not even with all these people swirling around.

With a deep sense of resignation and defeat, I rummaged around in my handbag, pulled out the phone, and mentally prepared to tell Grace I couldn't get her cassette player with the reason—the ghost of Old Betty.

My index finger pressed the ON button without hesitation. The phone flickered into life. Mark Twain's quote flashed across the screen:

"Do the thing you fear most and the death of fear is certain."

More tears welled in my eyes as I read and re-read the quote. Each tear wiped away seemed to fortify and give a quiet determination to continue; to keep doing that one thing I do well—to investigate until it fully exposes the truth.

I dropped the phone back in my handbag, buried my head in my hands, and stood there for some time, thinking hard. After several minutes, I looked up. "When you're given lemons, make lemonade," I said as a plan formed. "Doris, right here is an opportunity to help out your friend, and do a little research into Old Betty."

Pete Brown mentioned that Emily Johnson was a local historian. She was at the top of my list of people to speak with. But first I'd go to the *Lincolnshire Weekly News* archives area and get Grace's cassette player. Hadn't Jenny mentioned the archives contained photographs of the housekeeper? I'd use the visit to dig a little into the history of Old Betty.

"Might as well jot down a few notes for my article," I whispered under my breath.

The thought of entering that part of the museum sent a chilling shiver down my spine. But at least the museum was so busy there'd be skeleton hunters in every corner. If anything happened, my screams would bring them running, if not to help, to discover what happened.

"Doris, Old Gal, over here!"

My head snapped up, body erect, eyes instantly alert.

Captain Honeybush raised his cane as if greeting an old friend, then began to pick his way through the crowd.

I waited for a moment, uncertain as what to do next. Then with the speed of a hummingbird, darted into the throng, merging with the excited skeleton hunters. After several minutes of hurried steps, I turned around but didn't see the captain. Then thinking about returning to the archives area, my nerve failed. I simply couldn't go back to that place. Not tonight, anyway.

"Maybe tomorrow when it is daylight. Yes, that is what I'll do. Time to go home."

Straining my eyes for the exit, I thought I recognised a face on the far side of the lobby by the stairs. The face turned briefly in my direction, then away.

It was him!

The man with oversized hands who I'd danced with on the beach. I remembered his name—Mr Christy. He wore a dark undertaker's suit. And he looked decidedly furtive.

For several moments I watched as he eased his way through the crowd, his oversized hands flapping by his side like flags fluttering in a stiff breeze. Maybe it was in the nervous darting turn of the head or the hurried, jerky movement, but something about the man triggered my journalistic instinct.

Where was he going?

And why?

Chapter 49

THE SOUND OF EXCITED chatter drowned out the clop-clop of my shoes on the hard museum floor. With some difficulty I elbowed my way through the throng, muttering apologies. At the staircase that led to the second floor, I was right behind Mr Christy. He moved in little jerky spurts as if rust filled his joints. He was up to something, and I was close enough to see what it was.

As we wandered through the great hall on the second floor, I hung back a few paces hoping he wouldn't spin around. He turned off into a side room. I was about to follow, but a stout woman with frowning eyes, in a black, ankle-length, hooded robe, came from nowhere.

"Booo-hooo-booo!" she cried, spinning in little circles, her voice as harsh as her hair, which was cut almost to a bristle at the back. "Booo-hooo-booo!"

I shoved by the actress, without a word.

"Hey, you're supposed to scream for admission," she said in a squeal of indignation. "You'll have to do better than that inside else I won't get paid."

"Okay, next time I'll do better," I said.

Mr Christy, in the shadow of a display case, turned. The brow on his huge, square block-iron head wrinkled into deep corrugations. But if he recognized me, it didn't register in his eyes. Then he turned back and continued his grim march.

I had to hurry not to lose sight of him. A dim orange glow lit the room. It was full of I.A. Channer statues. Mostly adults with faces so real they gave me the creeps. In the centre, long rows of chairs faced towards a raised platform on which rested a large Egyptian-style sarcophagus. In the gloom I could just make out the edges of the ornate, boxlike funeral vessel. With a start, I realised there were people sitting in the chairs: mannequins at a funeral, I thought with a shiver—and hundreds of them.

With quick steps I hurried by a figure dressed in flowing robes, with a huge tabla drum under one arm. Next to him, with golden skin, stood two humanlike griffins. And behind them, five figures wearing the uniform of Victorian policemen.

"The teeth," I mumbled as I followed. "All Hollywood perfect."

But I was moving too fast to check that fact.

Mr Christy made a sharp left, picked up his pace, and hurried into a darkened corner. He stopped in front of an exhibit. The dim outline of a statuesque figure slowly formed as my eyes adjusted to the gloom.

It seemed this area was empty of visitors. Almost as if we were on a deserted island. Mr Christy reached out a hand, touched the figure on the shoulder and let out a chuckle.

From where I stood, Mr Christy's back blocked much of the view. Yet I could tell the mannequin was short and carried something in its hand.

With a start, I realised it was the statue of a child. I stood there staring straight ahead at the figure, sweat blooming in my armpits.

Then came the mumbled voice of Mr Christy. "Thank God I got here just in time to check." The large man stepped to one side and let out a deep-chested laugh. "Wonderful! Your soft skin glows just like a baby's."

And suddenly I saw the mannequin.

It was that of a boy.

In his right hand he carried an orange bucket and spade.

I let out a startled gasp.

"Tommy Peachtree!"

Chapter 50

THE FIGURE WAS THE spitting image of Tommy Peachtree. No! It was more than that, an exact replica, lifelike in all the details, including the scar above his right eyebrow. I stood there for a moment, uncertain what to do as a kind of tension began to creep over my body. With immense effort, I stepped forward, then another little step, placing my feet quietly one in front of the other until I was almost upon Mr Christy and the figure.

A boom caused me to spin around. The figure dressed in flowing robes had sprung to life, his thick hands beat the tabla drum in a frenzied rhythm. At his side, the two golden-skinned griffins boogied. When I turned back, Tommy Peachtree was dancing his way to the centre of the room, along with Mr Christy, whose large hands were raised high above his head. In an instant, there was a flash mob-style procession of dancing figures. They drifted towards the sarcophagus.

More mannequins sprung from nowhere, all waving arms and shouts. "Booo-hooo-booo!"

A short, skinny man with a bald head and protruding eyes led the way. His long, black cape flapped like a curtain in an open window. In his left hand he carried a mannequin's head daubed with red splotches. A man dressed as a seagull with thick feathered boards for wings twirled in a circle. I recognised the stout woman with frowning eyes in the black, ankle-length, hooded robe. There too, as part of the procession, was Pete Brown.

Members of the public poured into the room. Shouts of excitement filled the still air. In less than a minute the place was jam packed. Zombies danced. Children squealed. Grandparents bopped, and parents laughed.

The stout woman with the frowning eyes clambered onto the stage. "Booo-hooo-booo!" she cried, raising her hands.

The audience and dancing mannequins all responded. "Booo-hooo-booo!"

Then all of a sudden the drumming stopped, and the figures froze.

A nervous silence fell over the room as everyone looked in every direction eager to see what would happen next.

Footsteps.

Again, came the drumming.

Mr Channer sprinted into the room with his arms wide open and top-hat candles flashing. The Victorian police officers sprung to life. They chased after the artist with little real intent.

Mr Channer clambered onto the stage, opened the lid of the sarcophagus, waved his cape and yelled, "They'll never find me in here!"

The crowd cheered.

At that precise moment, Constable Wriggly entered the room. Unaware of the sudden surge of flashing camera lights, he drew his nightstick and charged towards the sarcophagus, eyes fixed and serious on Mr Channer.

Chapter 51

MRS LINTOTT LET THE kettle boil, poured out two mugs of tea, added milk and sugar, and sat down at her kitchen table with a plate full of fancy biscuits. It was almost midnight, and neither of us was ready to sleep.

"Oooh, Doris, to think, the whole thing was a publicity stunt!"

I blew on the surface of my mug. "So it seems."

"Not that I'm one to spread gossip, but what were we supposed to think when Mr Channer disappeared from town?"

I shrugged. "That he was guilty of something."

"Exactly," squawked Mrs Lintott, with the disgust of a sparrow denied an oversized worm. "And the whole thing was nothing more than a carefully crafted plan to drum up publicity for his gruesome exhibition!"

I stirred a teaspoon of sugar into my cup. "And it worked. I don't think it was possible to squeeze any more people into the Beachside Museum tonight."

Mrs Lintott's nose wrinkled in annoyance. "Oh, the cheek of it! I hope they charge Mr Channer for wasting police time."

I thought about that for a moment and said, "The Skegness police station won't want any more negative publicity about the Dancing Hands Mystery."

"Yes, love, you are right about that. They'll let this drop and hope it goes away. But me and my bingo ladies will talk about it for years to come."

I said, "You've got to admire Mr Channer, at least for putting on a good show."

"Oh yes, love. Some of the exhibits sent a chill up my spine. I went into one room and felt a blast of cold air, heard chains rattling, and saw swirls of mist. I didn't hang around, I can tell you that."

My body tensed. "A blast of cold air and chains rattling?"

"That's right, love."

Instantly alert I said, "Which part of the museum were you in?"

"Don't know, love. That place is massive. I was with Nurse Phillips and Mrs McLaughlin, in an archives area of some sort. A figure in black appeared out of thin air wailing like the devil himself. It reminded me a little of the magic act Mr Channer used to perform years back—all spooky and gruesome with everything in black."

"That's it!" I said, realizing my experience in the archives room must have been part of the show. It was all right. There was no ghost. No ghost, that is, of Old Betty—only the exhibits and I.A. Channer's magic act. "It wasn't Old Betty after all, just a magician's illusion!"

"What are you talking about, love?"

Tilting my head back I let out a relieved laugh. There was little point explaining my foolish mistake, so I changed the subject. "I feel sorry for Constable Wriggly."

"Oooh, Doris, me too." Mrs Lintott's voice rose to an excited warble. "The man's already got egg on his face over losing the body of Fiona Fenchurch in broad daylight all those years ago. I felt sorry for him then as well."

"So the Dancing Hands Mystery remains unsolved?"

"That's right. Poor Constable Wriggly." Mrs Lintott's voice took on a merry chirp. "And now with all those photographs of him chasing Mr Channer in the Beachside Museum. Oh dear, it won't look good to see a Skegness police officer in uniform surrounded by dancing zombies in the newspaper. Oh no. Especially the shots where he attempted to arrest poor innocent Mr Channer as he lay in the Egyptian sarcophagus."

I said, "Let's hope the photographs don't see the light of day for Constable Wriggly's sake."

Mrs Lintott clapped her hands, her voice twittered with the melodic chirp of a satisfied sparrow. "This is the digital age. My bingo ladies Facebook group are already sharing shots. Soon the photos will be all over the internet. Mark my words."

"Oh dear!" I felt sorry for the officer, but there was little I could do to help.

Mrs Lintott shook her head in a long slow motion. "What is this world coming to? Tonight's events make our police look like buffoons. And Constable Wriggly's bound to be a laughing stock, poor lamb. I feel so sorry for him."

I said, "This will wash over in a few weeks."

Mrs Lintott tapped a finger on her mug. "Love, this isn't London. People in town have long memories; Constable Wriggly will never live this down." She let out a sad sigh. It was a little too long to be genuine. "It has doomed the poor fellow to walk the beat in uniform for the rest of his career. He's like a haunted policeman. Me and the bingo ladies will talk about it, as a way to help, but what he needs is a miracle."

As I thought about that, I wondered aloud. "Like explaining how the body of Fiona Fenchurch ended up in the Beachside Museum?"

"It'll take more than that now, love. Constable Wriggly's only hope is to solve the Dancing Hands Mystery in full. No loose ends. That'll never happen." Again, Mrs Lintott shook her head. "Not that I know about these things, but you ought to write an article about it. I'm sure it would sell."

For several moments I stared into my mug, the wheels of my mind churning. Then I looked up at Mrs Lintott, smiled and said, "Yes, I will."

Chapter 52

THE FOLLOWING MORNING, I was up at eight, showered, and caffeinated by eight thirty and staring into my laptop computer screen by nine. I'd decided to spend the morning scouring the internet for jobs. Since I'd told Grace the town was littered with undiscovered vacancies, I felt I should uncover at least a dozen or so. The plan was simple—once I'd compiled an extensive list, I'd send it over to her. I was determined to search the internet until I'd found them. There was no way I would let her down.

Anyone who has looked for a job online knows well enough the sense of anticipation at the start of a search. The internet brings with it a sense of infinite opportunity. There is no telling what nuggets of gold you will uncover. With this mood of optimism, I began my hunt.

With rapid clicks of the mouse, quick taps on the keyboard, I opened websites, stared hard at the offerings and scrolled to read the details. Fuelled by a good night's sleep and caffeine, I moved with speed from site to site.

After almost two hours crouched over my laptop, I stood up and let out an exasperated sigh. Exactly one job vacancy—security guard at the Beachside Museum.

"Oh bugger!"

I got up, made a cup of coffee, and sat back down at the kitchen table, eyes staring blankly at the laptop screen. For ten minutes, I simply sat there, speechless, my forehead growing slowly damp with sweat, my mind spinning with indecision.

It was the sounds of activity in the street below that brought me back to the present.

"Time for a different direction."

I closed the laptop, picked up my mobile phone, scrolled through my contacts and sent Jenny Styles a message:

Did you speak with the editor of the Lincolnshire Weekly News, *Marcus Baker, about my article on Old Betty?*

Her reply was almost instant:

Yes, I mentioned you and your article. Marcus is rather busy all the time, but at least he listened. Even better, he would like to talk to you! Strike while the iron's hot. Call him now— telephone number below.

01754 619 0735

Good luck.

Your biggest fan cheering you on,

Jenny.

I picked up my mobile phone and typed in the numbers. A woman's voice answered on the first ring.

"Good morning, this is Miss Timothy at the *Lincolnshire Weekly News*. I'm Mr Marcus Baker's personal secretary. How may I assist you today?"

I said, "Please put me through to Mr Baker; he is expecting my call."

"And you are?" The words were friendly enough, but the tone was as sour as an unripe lemon.

"Oh, I'm sorry. Doris Cudlow, Mrs."

The vinegary voice said, "And what is the exact nature of your call?"

The woman's tone was so off-putting, I said, "He is expecting to hear from me."

"I see." There was a long pause where I thought I heard the rustling of paper. "I don't see any appointments in his diary under your name; did you say he was expecting your call?"

"Oh, we didn't have a formal appointment."

"Really?" The single word came out as if she'd sipped from a glass of soured milk.

"A friend of Mr Baker asked me to call."

After a long vinegary pause the woman said, "Mr Baker is a busy man and never takes telephone calls at random from salespeople." She drew out the last word long and slow, as if she were a doctor removing pus from an infected wound.

"I'm not a salesperson."

"Then what exactly is the nature of your business?"

This was getting nowhere, so I said, "Mr Baker is interested in an article. I'm a freelance journalist."

"Ah!" The word hung in the air like a bad smell. "I see, so you want to sell Mr Baker a feature, eh?"

The question pushed me in a corner. I didn't want to say yes and sound like a sleazy salesperson, but I needed to speak with Mr Baker. I picked up my coffee cup, put it back down without drinking and said, "Yes, that's right."

"So you are a salesperson, aren't you?" There was a twinkle of acerbic triumph in her voice.

"Well, I suppose so." Then I quickly added. "He is expecting my call. Can you put me through?"

"No." The word came out suddenly, like a crack of thunder of an unseen summer storm.

"Pardon?"

"Did I not make myself clear? Mr Baker is way too busy to take unsolicited calls from salespeople." Again, she said the last word as if it was something nasty.

I took in a sharp breath, let the air out slowly and said, "Can I leave a message?"

The line went quiet for so long I thought she had hung up. At last, she said, "Tell me what the article is about, and I'll pass on a memo."

I gave Miss Timothy the details, crossed my fingers, and hoped the message would get through. But no matter how optimistic I tried to feel, I felt sure nothing would come of it.

After I hung up I stared at my half-drunk cup of coffee and said, "Whether or not Mr Baker gets the memo, I will write that article!"

But somehow, I knew for that to be true, I must begin at once. The first stage of a journalistic piece, no matter the subject, is research. And it is always easier to start with a personal interview. Conversations with people who know a little about a subject can spark further questions and ideas. I thought back to the events at the museum yesterday evening and chided myself for not speaking with Emily Johnson. I felt sure her knowledge of local history would prove invaluable to my article.

"Clean forgot with all the excitement."

Pete Brown mentioned her as the head librarian at the Skegness Grammar School. Again, I reached for my phone, did an internet search and dialled.

A mechanical voice answered on the second ring.

"Welcome to the Skegness Grammar School information line. The administrative offices are closed today for staff training. Please call back tomorrow. Goodbye."

I didn't know what to think. It was still morning, and it seemed at every turn there was nothing but dead ends. No jobs, no cosy chat with Mr Baker, and no Emily Johnson at the grammar school.

I took a sip from my cup. The coffee was cold.

"Maybe I should give up and go back to bed!"

It was then I remembered Grace River's old-fashioned cassette recorder and my promise to get it from the Beachside Museum. With little else to do, other than stare at the walls of my tiny bedsit apartment, I stood up, picked up my handbag, and headed out of the door.

Chapter 53

A WARM MIDDAY BREEZE swept in from the sea as I hurried to the entrance of the Beachside Museum. The car park, almost empty, was a world away from the hustle and bustle of the previous evening. There were no police officers directing traffic, no crowds converging on the main doors, and no air of excitement about the place. The atmosphere was still, almost mausoleum silent.

A handwritten sign hung at an angle on the main door. SORRY CLOSED TO THE PUBLIC.

I checked the time on my phone—a little after midday.

"The museum should be open by now."

A strange mixture of relief and frustration filled my body; on the one hand, I didn't want to return to the *Lincolnshire Weekly News* archives even though I'd figured out there was no ghost. On the other, I'd promised Grace I'd get her tape cassette recorder, and I wanted to keep the momentum in my research into Old Betty.

Ignoring the sign, I tried the door handle. It didn't move.

Not wanting to give up, I leaned against the windowpane and peered through the glass. The main lobby was dimly lit. At the reception desk sat a uniformed figure, head down as if reading. I recognised her, even from this distance—Alicia Osborn.

I banged on the glass door, hard. Then again, and again.

Alicia's head shot up. An instant later, she was on her feet, hurrying to the front door. As she got close, she slowed a little, then as recognition flashed in her eyes, picked up her pace.

"Hi, Doris, the museum is closed today," she said, opening the door.

I smiled and said, "Why?"

"A museum board directive, so the building can stay open longer tonight."

"For the I.A. Channer exhibition?"

Alicia nodded. "Several buses are coming over from Lincoln. Tickets are sold out for tonight's show. There is even a television news crew visiting later."

"Is that so?"

Alicia tugged at a lock of hair. "Oh yes. The actors will be here as well. The word on the beach is that a large museum in London is considering Mr Channer's exhibition for spring next year."

I said, "So the museum is closed until tonight?"

"That's right."

It looked like a wasted journey, but I didn't want to give up. I thought back to the Positive Outcomes journalism course I'd taken several years ago in London. Taught by an orange-tanned, pearly-white-toothed Californian who'd settled in the London borough of Ealing, it offered three sure-fire techniques for influencing people to say "Yes."

"Before I share these secret techniques," the instructor had said in his Los Angeles accent, "understand they only work if you stay calm, then they are like pure nuggets of gold. But lose your temper and they turn to dust!"

I deployed the first technique: "Sugar Coating" and said, "You must be exhausted after such a long shift?"

"That's right, and it's a triple—sixteen hours straight. I'm just about hanging on, but I need the money. The credit card company will repossess my car if I don't make payment next week. Where would I be without a car? The pay from this job will just about cover it and my rent. But yes, I'm exhausted."

There was no point beating about the bush, so I moved to the second technique: "Ask for What You Want" and said, "I'm really here to use the *Lincolnshire Weekly News* archives. I'm writing an article on the former housekeeper of the museum. Do you think I could have a quick look around?"

Alicia glanced back over her shoulder and lowered her voice to a whisper. "Sure, come in."

Chapter 54

"DORIS, I'VE GOT TO remain at the main reception area because the closed-circuit television system is out of order," said Alicia as we walked into the lobby. "Are you okay making your way to the archives area?"

"Absolutely."

"Good. Now whatever you do, please don't let Captain Honeybush see you. He said he'll fire me on the spot if I let anyone in the building without his permission."

"I'll be as quiet as a church mouse. Have you seen him?"

Alicia shrugged. "He's around somewhere, probably in his office in a drunken snooze."

"Perfect! I'll be discreet. You can count on me." A concerned thought entered my mind. Uncertain how to express it, I said, "Did the captain give you any problems last night?"

Alicia grinned. "Oh no. Miss Jenny Styles called to say she put a little something in his nightcap. No idea what it was, but I haven't seen the captain since the museum closed."

An urgent buzz came from my handbag. I pulled out my mobile phone, glanced at the screen but didn't recognise the number.

"Well, hello, Mrs Cudlow, this is your friend Marcus Baker from the *Lincolnshire Weekly News*."

I almost dropped the phone and stammered, "Mr Baker?"

"That's right. Jenny Styles told me all about you and your idea for an article on Old Betty. I love it! The answer is yes, yes, and yes."

"Oh my gosh," I said in shock. "Oh my goodness."

Alicia glanced in my direction, concern filling her eyes.

I gave her the thumbs-up, and she nodded.

Mr Baker said, "Can you get your article to me by Friday next week?"

Without hesitation I said, "Yes, I can do that."

"Wonderful. I'm off to an organic yurt camp in Barbados in an hour or so. I'll look forward to reading your article when I get back. Now, is there anything else you'd like to ask while you have me on the line?"

Thinking about my finances I said, "Do you pay by bank transfer or paper cheque?"

"Whatever you prefer, Mrs Cudlow. My secretary, Miss Timothy, will be in contact with the finer details of the contract. Please provide her with all the information requested. She prefers text messages; is this number good?"

"Yes," the word came out breathless. My head spun with joy.

Mr Baker continued, "Mrs Cudlow, I hear you worked for the *Skegness Telegraph*, good newspaper; sorry it closed down. Where are you working now?"

I didn't want to say nowhere or that I'm a former doughnut fryer at Fantasy Gardens Amusement Arcade. "I've just finished a stint working as a security guard at the Beachside Museum." I held my breath.

"Perfect! You'll have access to the archives of the museum for your research. Why, I couldn't have wished for more. If the story goes down well, there will be additional freelance work along similar lines. Good reporters are hard to find. Welcome aboard."

When I hung up, I waved my hands in the air swaying from side to side like a tree in a spring breeze. "I've got a contract to write a story for the *Lincolnshire Weekly News*," I sang, and Alicia joined in the celebration.

Then I set off with confident strides towards the *Lincolnshire Weekly News* archives.

Chapter 55

AS I MADE MY WAY ALONG the vast corridors, up flights of stairs, and past large exhibits, I suddenly had the feeling I was being watched. I stopped, and in a slow movement, did a three hundred and sixty degree turn.

The dimmed overhead lights illuminated particles of dust drifting aimlessly in the still air. Display cases stretched off in every direction, and an I.A. Channer figure of a woman in a large, yellow, floppy hat walked a panting English bulldog. Other than that, there was no one else in this area of the museum, and it was deserted and almost uncannily still. A closed-circuit television hung motionless high on a far wall, but Alicia mentioned the system was out of order, and its little red light was out.

"There isn't anyone watching."

Slowly, with care, as if walking to my bedsit bathroom without disturbing Mr Pandy, I continued my journey. But as I headed towards the hallway that led to the *Lincolnshire Weekly* archives, again I had the inexorable sensation of being watched.

A sharp hum caused me to jump. I spun around as the sound continued. It came from my handbag—the phone, a text message.

Dear Mrs Cudlow,

I have been informed you are to supply the newspaper with an article. Before we can formally accept your item, we need a reference from your last paid employment. Mr Baker mentioned you work as a security guard at the Beachside Museum. The head of security is a Captain Honeybush, I believe? Please have the gentleman supply a reference. If his assessment is acceptable, I will send you over the terms and conditions along with a contract.

Yours Sincerely,

Miss Timothy.

My stomach roiled at the thought of approaching Captain Honeybush for a reference. I re-read the message, then thinking about the situation fought a massive lump in my throat, not knowing if I should call Miss Timothy or let it lie for a while whilst I thought about what to do. After a long moment I let out a low groan and dialled.

Miss Timothy picked up on the first ring. "Good morning, this is Miss Timothy at the *Lincolnshire Weekly News*. I'm Mr Marcus Baker's personal secretary. How may I assist you today?"

"Hello, Miss Timothy, this is Doris Cudlow. I hope you are well this bright and sunny afternoon."

There was a long silence, then in an acerbic voice, she said, "What is it you want to sell?"

I put on my let's be friends tone and said, "Thank you for the text message. It is such—"

"Don't thank me," interrupted Miss Timothy. "It is Mr Baker who believes random salespeople are fit to write for our treasured newspaper." She sniffed. "It seems my opinion on the matter is inconsequential."

Mind racing to shift the conversation on to more helpful ground, I thought back to the Positive Outcomes journalism course for influencing people to say "Yes." I took a deep breath to calm my mind, then as I exhaled, I used the first technique: "Sugar Coating," and I said, "Do you know, the personal secretary is one of the most important people in a corporation?"

"Mrs Cudlow, do you know I've worked here for twenty years, and you're the first person to acknowledge that important fact?" There was a hint of warmth in Miss Timothy's voice. "I've been a reader of our beloved newspaper since I was seven. I won't see fifty again. Now, how can I help you today?"

There was no point beating about the bush, so I moved to the second technique: "Ask for What You Want" and said, "I wonder if I might use an alternative reference?"

"Why?"

"The fact is I was working at the museum to help a friend."

"I see."

"And it was only for a couple of nights."

"Well, this is rather unusual. What was your last place of employment?"

My mouth spluttered the answer before my brain could stop it. "Fantasy Gardens Amusement Arcade."

A slight tartness entered her voice. "Doing what?"

I hesitated for a moment, realised there was little point in obfuscation and said as positively as possible, "Doughnut fryer, but I worked as a reporter at—"

"No."

I continued speaking. "The *Skegness Telegraph*. How about I request a reference from my old boss, at the newspaper?"

"I said no!"

There was an immovable finality in her voice, so I tried the third technique: "Elevate to a Higher Authority" and said, "Can you put me through to Mr Baker?"

Miss Timothy's voice turned as cold as a January sub-zero gust. "I'll not let the likes of you go creeping behind my back to my boss."

"I just want to clarify a few points around the—"

"No." The word came out like a blast of frigid air.

Anger and frustration fired every muscle as I yelled, "This is beyond ridiculous. This is absolutely absurd. Put me through to Mr Baker, right now!"

Miss Timothy hissed, "Company policy requires a reference from your last employer. Please have Captain Honeybush supply a statement as to the integrity of your character and professionalism of your work by Friday."

"But—"

"Mrs Cudlow, I need not remind you that newspapers run to tight deadlines. If the reference is not forthcoming, we shall have to fill the pages with material supplied by our in-house journalists rather than cooks at fat-frying outlets."

Click.

"Oh bugger!"

Still clutching the phone tight in my hand, I trudged with weary feet along the length of the hallway towards the *Lincolnshire Weekly* archives.

"If only I'd known that the day would turn out like this, I'd have stayed in bed."

Besides the closed door to the tiny reception area, I considered my next steps. There was no moving Miss Timothy. That left Captain Honeybush. And there was no possibility of approaching that odious man. I was stuck... unless I directly connected with Mr Baker, but he was probably on his way to the airport and an exotic holiday in Barbados.

Something sharp tapped my shoulder.

I spun around and shouted, "Hey!"

A thin woman—emaciated would be more accurate—and somewhat stooped, pointed at the closed door to the archives lobby. She wore a Beachside Museum security guard uniform, with an oversized cap tipped forward, shielding her eyes.

"The archives are closed!" Her voice sounded like the crackle of mist rising from a cold sea.

"Who are you?" I demanded, gripping even tighter on to my phone. "I didn't realise there was another security officer patrolling this area."

She ignored my question. "Did the captain send you?"

The earlier warning about Captain Honeybush put me on high alert. I didn't want him to know I was here—it would cost Alicia her job. "Captain is snoozing; I work security here."

The woman stood very still for a moment as if frozen in ice, but I could feel her eyes looking at me, although they were hidden by the tip of her cap. "You are here to take over, aren't you?"

I shook my head. "Not exactly, but I—"

"Good, doors unlocked. It has been a long wait; this place is spooky. Please keep the reception door shut: Captain's orders." She turned and hurried away.

I glanced at the door handle, then back towards the woman. She was gone, probably headed down the staircase back to the main lobby and car park. Maybe I'd see her again, but the finality of her words left me uncertain.

"Damn right about the spooky part," I muttered under my breath, turning the door handle. With every ounce of willpower, I pushed and urged my legs to carry me into what felt like a dark, gloomy chasm.

Instinctively my hand reached for the light switch. To my surprise they came on with a click, bathing the windowless room in bright white light.

It was just as I remembered it. The windowless walls, the clock above the doorjamb, the reception desk with the door beyond, which led into the central archives.

"No I.A. Channer figures!"

I felt a wash of relief pour over my body, lifting my mood. Then it surged with an unexpected thud of confidence.

"I'll check the archives for information on Old Betty then grab Grace's cassette player on the way out."

With determined steps I hurried to the main archives door, hesitating for only a moment to bolster my courage. Then I pushed and entered without waiting a second longer.

Even with the light from the open door, it took half a minute for my eyes to adjust and the gloom to recede into the shadows. The hum of the electric lights pulsated, at one moment soft, the next high pitched like the buzz of an angry bee. Unhurried, I studied the aisle of shelves near the door. They were packed with boxes and folders; some were half-open with papers bulging out.

Gripped by a sudden urge, I walked along the aisle, slowing my steps in front of a stack of yellowed newspapers placed in a neat pile on a shelf at eye level. Something about their order in a sea of chaos attracted my attention. It was as if someone had taken the time to organise the pile while leaving the rest of the shelf untouched.

I picked up the top newspaper, opening it out to read the headline. It was from ten years ago.

Body Disappears from Beach During Festival

"Authorities have released the identity of the body that disappeared under police guard during this year's Retirees' Spring Festival. Fiona Fenchurch was murdered while dancing on the Skegness beach, surrounded by hundreds of festivalgoers."

A tremor of excitement fluttered through my body. It was as if the newspaper was some sort of message. But from who?

I continued to read, straining my eyes in the dim light.

"Eyewitnesses say the body disappeared while a police constable was being treated for sunstroke by a local nurse. A former military officer who helped maintain order during the initial chaos is quoted as saying, "One moment the body was there, the next it was gone." The authorities have asked Judge Eboch to lead an investigation into the..."

The archives door snapped shut with a sudden thwack.

I jumped, glanced around but saw no one.

"Don't be silly, Doris. Nothing to worry about here. Nothing to fear at all. Just do a little research, snap some photos, write some notes, grab Grace's tape recorder, and get the hell out of here."

Chapter 56

AS I HURRIED TO SNAP photographs of the newspaper, I thought about Fiona Fenchurch and knew it would interest Mr Baker.

"A feature article about the discovery of her body, tied in with the history of the building and Old Betty!"

The idea stuck in my mind as I continued to leaf through the yellowed pages. I'd have to come up with a plan to get around Miss Timothy's insistence on a reference from Captain Honeybush.

"Where there's a will, there's a way."

I placed the newspaper back on the stack, mentally noted the location, then scrolled through the images captured by my phone. Satisfied with their quality and trembling with fear and anticipation, I walked to the back of the archives area stopping at the fifth door—the room where I discovered Fiona Fenchurch's body.

My heart hammered against my chest like a train behind schedule as I stared at the handle. It was like the others along this wall: small, metal, with one of those old-fashioned locks that took a long cylindrical key. There was no police tape or anything else to show the gruesome reality of the room.

"Probably locked," I said, half hoping that to be true.

With a quick twist of the handle, the door creaked open. A blast of musty air almost turned me away, but I was determined to take photographs of the space and jot down any observations.

I reached a hand into the room for the light switch before stepping inside. The air was cooler, the lingering smell of disinfectant, polish, and soap permeated the mustiness of the space. For a moment I stood in the stillness then pulled a box from a shelf and wedged the door open, glancing up at the small cracked mirror that hung near the door.

After ten minutes, I had all the photographs I needed. I let out a long sigh and asked the one question that filled my mind.

"How could Fiona's remains have lain undetected in this room?"

It amazed me that a body could lie only half concealed for any length of time in this small, dingy chamber. You would have thought with all the comings and goings of the museum security officers that a human body would have been noticed.

But no.

There had to be something else, something I was missing. With my journalistic instincts on high alert, I thought about Fred Faul. He had said he patrolled this room every shift. Then I thought of his idle nature, thought of his drunkenness, thought of the boxes that only half hid the body, and decided he couldn't have entered this room. And that, I knew, was a key piece of the puzzle to the mystery.

I took a long moment to think about it all.

With a start, I recalled the instructions from Captain Honeybush relayed by Jenny as we sat together in the reception on my first night as a security guard. "The archives area is behind that door.

There is the main room and four or five smaller spaces at the back. No need to patrol those: Captain's orders."

Tap-tap-tap.

The sound caused me to glance towards the open door. As I did so, and out of the corner of my eye, something moved across the face of the cracked mirror. With a sharp turn of my head, I gazed at the glass.

The reflection that stared back wasn't mine.

A woman, stooped, with a black shawl thrown over rounded shoulders stared out through the cracked mirror glass. In one hand she held a broom, in the other a large cylindrical key. But it was her face that caused my heart to pound so hard it almost broke free from my chest.

It was nothing but shade.

Chapter 57

NOT EVEN THE MOST FEARFUL thoughts, not even the most exaggerated of all my fevered imaginings, had prepared me for anything like this. I screamed, stumbled against the mirror, and ran.

The ear-splitting sound as the frame tumbled to the floor was drowned out by another noise.

Tap-tap-tap.

Tap-tap-tap.

Tap-tap-tap.

I ran along the main aisle and hit something soft and warm, infused with tobacco and alcohol. Arms wrapped around, drawing me close.

"Steady on, Old Gal."

I took a ragged breath and turned my head upward into the annoyed glare of Captain Honeybush. He stood rooted to the spot, his tiny, brown eyes searching my face. When he spoke, it was in a low growl. "What the dickens is going on here?"

"Get away from me," I cried as I wriggled out of his embrace. My terrified mind could barely function. It ordered my legs to run, but they trembled too much to move.

The captain shot out his left hand, grasped my wrist, his eyes drifting to the little rooms at the back of the archives. Then he turned his full attention on me. "Mrs Cudlow, I said, what is going on here?"

Unable to let out the shriek trapped in my throat my free hand darted into my handbag to grab my phone. I broke away from his grip, stumbled back into a stack of shelves, and squeezed the ON button. As the phone flickered into life, I said, "What the hell are you doing creeping about the archives?"

The captain just stood there, a half smile of derision on his face, peanut-sized eyes narrowed, cane in his right hand. With a slow motion he smoothed down the corners of his thin, waxed moustache with the thumb and forefinger of his left hand. "Mrs Cudlow, do I need to remind you I am the head of security. The real question is what are you doing in here when the facilities are closed to the public?"

I half turned towards the small storage room where the mirror lay shattered on the floor. Then I opened my mouth to explain but snapped it shut as the realisation of how it would sound dawned.

"Just as well I am diligent about my patrols," Captain Honeybush said, tapping his cane hard against the concrete floor. "Mrs Cudlow, it was your screams that caught my attention." He stepped closer. "Old Gal, you weren't snooping around those storage rooms again, were you?"

My mind churned, trying to make sense of it all and failing. "Err... I... well." And then suddenly, a strange calmness washed over me. My thoughts cleared. I said, "I read in an old newspaper that you helped guard the body of Fiona Fenchurch. Is that true?"

The captain smashed his cane hard against the floor, his breathing shallow and quick. "Those storage rooms are off limits to everyone but me!"

"What happened to Fiona Fenchurch that day on the beach?" The words came out of my mouth although I wasn't conscious of my lips moving.

He fell silent. I spoke again.

"What can you tell me about the Dancing Hands Mystery?"

The captain turned his head stiffly towards the rooms at the back of the archives. With a laboured movement he rubbed his chin. His mouth opened, and I thought he was about to utter an answer to my question. Instead, he just gazed at the spot from where I had fled.

I tried again. "Did you see what happened?"

And now, at last, he growled out words. "I should call the police, have the museum prosecute you for trespassing."

A journalistic bloodhound instinct urged me to say, "Do you know how Fiona's body ended up in an archives storeroom?"

The captain's tiny eyes opened in rage. He barked, "Who let you into the building?" He didn't wait for an answer. "Alicia Osborn, eh? Well, this is her last day working for the Beachside Museum!"

Instantly, and as if galvanised by a protective instinct I said, "No, don't blame Alicia. It was a mistake!"

Captain Honeybush stepped closer. "Trespassing and entering! A mistake?"

"Listen, I can explain—"

Again, he stepped forward. The smell of stale tobacco and day-old alcohol assaulted my nostrils. It made my skin crawl. "Mrs Cudlow, did you enter the storage rooms?"

"Why would I do that?"

The captain's nostrils flared as he yelled, "Answer my question, damn it!"

I tried to stay calm and said in a soft voice, "Captain Honeybush, I find your tone and manner rather unpleasant."

With the rapidity of a light switch illuminating a darkened room, his voice softened to a low calculated tone. "Mrs Cudlow, I have something for you."

There was an ominous glint in his tiny eyes. I stepped backwards into the shelf and balled my fists. "Really?"

The captain's lips twisted into a sinister smile as he reached into his jacket pocket and pulled out a sheet of paper. "The bill for the damage you caused to the I.A. Channer exhibit. Seven hundred pounds. I wanted to give it to you yesterday evening, but I lost you in the crowd. Just as well I saw you today; it'll save me a stamp."

The captain waved the sheet of paper at eye level.

My hand stretched out automatically, and my mouth opened wide without my say-so. "Seven hundred pounds!" It might as well have been a million.

"Seven days to settle, else we'll have the debt collector seize your assets."

"What?" I'm no legal expert, but that seemed a little fast. "No way!"

"I'm afraid so. Why don't you check with a lawyer?" He let out a self-satisfied chuckle. "If you can afford one." There was something about his erect body language, confident tilt of the head, and gleam in the eyes that convinced me this was no idle threat.

"I don't have any money!"

"Do you have a car?"

"No, no... you can't take that... I... eh?"

The captain stepped back, spreading his legs wide like a Roman centurion. "If that is your only asset, you'll have to walk from now on, and I'm sure the judge will go easy on prison time for trespassing."

"Oh bugger!" My shoulders slumped.

The captain's lips tugged into a wolfish grin, and his eyes flashed as if he'd found the solution to a difficult problem. "Perhaps we can do a little deal, Mrs Cudlow."

I didn't like the curve of his lips or the leer in his brown eyes.

I said, "What type of deal?" It wasn't a question I wanted to ask, but there seemed no other logical response.

"I'll need to keep a close eye on you." The wolfish smile deepened. "The museum has a vacancy for a full-time security guard. I'd like to offer you the position. What do you say, Old Gal?"

I changed the subject to give my panicked mind time to think. "You fired Grace Rivers; why don't you offer the job to her?"

A cautious calculation flashed in his eyes. "Forgot you two are friends... makes sense. You are like two peas in a pod. Tell you what, Old Gal, Grace has her job back. I'll drop all charges, and I won't fire Alicia either... if you work as my full-time personal assistant." His sleazy emphasis on the word personal left little to the imagination.

Stunned, I shook my head, my mind blank. I needed more time to think but didn't have it. I said, "Do you have the power to grant all that?"

Captain Honeybush leaned against the cane and pulled out a hip flask. Staring vaguely into the dark shadows at the back of the archives he took a long slow swig. "I have the power to do what the hell I like. I could get away with murder, if I chose to."

"Murder!"

"Old boys' network, don't you know."

"I'm going to the police."

"Then I'll have to prosecute you for trespassing, call the debt collectors, take Grace to court, and fire Alicia. Judge Eboch is a dear friend. I'll have him throw the book at you!"

The rush of blood to my head was so blinding I had to lean against a shelf. "Oh my God!"

The captain licked his lips as he saw the flicker of hope extinguished from my eyes. He took two little triumphant steps forward, so close his breath wafted up my nostrils. It wasn't the freshest.

"Mrs Cudlow, how about you start as my personal assistant this Friday?"

Chapter 58

THAT NIGHT, BACK AT my bedsit, my sleep was restless and disturbed. More than once I got up, tiptoed across my room and stared out into the street below. Now at 2 a.m., the moon hid behind a dark cloud, underscoring a sense of bleakness that reflected my mood.

By the window, my eyes focused on the shadows, ears straining to hear the distinctive pistol crack of Captain Honeybush's cane on the pavement below. It didn't help that my bedsit apartment door didn't lock. At what point, exactly, did I stumble, like a housefly, into this tangled web from which there appeared no escape?

For the tenth time, I went over the situation, and for the tenth time, my rational brain offered the same answer—accept Captain Honeybush's offer.

And I had.

The moon met my mood, disappearing beneath a cloud in the bleak ashen night sky. It didn't help that in my hurry to get away from the *Lincolnshire Weekly* archives, I'd forgotten to get Grace's cassette recorder, or that I must tell her the only job on offer was at the Beachside Museum, on Captain Honeybush's terms.

Pushing the curtains farther aside, I leaned my hands against the windowpane, watching a slow procession of murky-looking clouds drift across the night sky.

"What I need is a plan. A damn good one. And before I start work this Friday."

The words echoed in the stillness of the room, triggering a new hope. It sparkled in my chest, so powerful I could savour the sweetness of escape from the captain's clutches. The solution was within reach, on the tip of my tongue. But somehow, when it came to the details, there was nothing in my head other than to stay far out of the odious man's reach.

It was all I had.

I didn't like it.

For a long while, I stared at the sky, letting my mind empty.

Tiptoeing to the bathroom, as I had done so often, I paused for a moment as the embryo of an idea flashed across my mind. It was gone before it formed shape, consumed by fevered thoughts of dread.

I took a long hot shower. There is something in the steam, the heat, and the soapy scents that always relaxes my body and frees my mind to generate ideas. Now I hoped to pull into my head that lost flash of inspiration. In it, I sensed, lay the key to this whole mess. I stood for a long while in the steaming water, as if it were rinsing away more than the grime of the day, as if it were washing away the acceptance of Captain Honeybush's offer, and opening up the doorway to a solution.

When the water ran cold, my shoulders slumped as if weighted down by defeat. There were no new ideas, no new insights, only the emptiness of barren winds that ravage a fallen city.

I needed a drink—a strong one.

At the fridge, I pulled out the six-pack. One by one I opened and drank. It was 4 a.m. when I tossed the last can into the dustbin.

My mind still raced.

Alcohol wasn't enough.

Staggering to my feet, I shuffled to the bathroom.

Thud, thud, thud.

"Sorry, Mr Pandy. Emergency bathroom visit—you know how that is." The words came out slurred. I felt dizzy.

In the bathroom, I glanced into the cabinet mirror, half expecting to see a ghostly face stare back. There was nothing but the image of a middle-aged, red-eyed woman at the end of her tether. As I stared into my reflection, I wondered if I knew the person looking back at me.

Casting my eyes away from the mirrored glass, I opened the cabinet door, took out the sleeping pill bottle, shook out two tablets, and swallowed.

Yes, I was using the drink and pills to run away.

But at this late hour, when sleep wouldn't come, I was too tired to care.

Chapter 59

AT NINE O'CLOCK THE next morning, Thursday, my eyes snapped open. I had no excuse for waking this early. The bright morning light glittered at the edges of the curtains, and I knew at once it was another sunny day. With dismay, I realised there was little to drag me out of bed. Only the dreaded phone call to Grace Rivers, and a whole day to think about my working for Captain Honeybush at the Beachside Museum. Then there was a late afternoon meal with Jenny Styles in the Fiddlers Bowl Café, but that wasn't until four.

Lying still, pushing thoughts of the day away, I said, "Less than five hours sleep, Doris. Go back to snooze land."

I put my head down on the pillow, pulled the covers over my head, and squeezed my eyes tight shut.

Nothing.

I was wide awake and as alert as if I'd drunk a pot of coffee.

I sat up. The first thing I expected to form was a headache. The second was a wave of disgust-fuelled depression.

I felt neither.

Instead, as I gazed at the bands of light dancing at the edge of the curtains, my mind cleared and then filled with the germ of an idea. It developed slowly, tapping at my subconscious mind like Captain Honeybush's cane.

"Best lance the boil, and be done with it."

I rolled over, grabbed a notepad and pen, and wrote down a list of things I needed to do. Then I put the kettle on to boil, made a cup of instant coffee and sipped it, black. After the second cup, I added to the list and prepared myself for a day of action.

Top of the list—Skegness Grammar School. It was time to speak with Emily Johnson. Pete Brown mentioned she was the head librarian, and I needed to pick her brain about a little local history.

"No time like the present," I said to the empty room as I picked up my mobile phone and dialled. I crossed my fingers, hoping the staff weren't on another administrative training day.

"Skegness Grammar School," said an efficient female voice after the first ring. "How can I help you today?"

"Can you put me through to the head librarian?"

"She is out right now. Do you want me to transfer you to voice mail?"

I thought about that for an instant. "No. Do you know when she will be in school?"

There was a pause followed by the clicks of a keyboard. "Around eleven. Would you like me to schedule you in for a call?"

"I'd rather visit."

Another pause. "Yes, I can do that. Can I have your name?"

I gave her my details.

"Please bring photo identification with you, and show it to whoever is manning the main reception desk."

Chapter 60

THE SUN WAS UP OVER the sea now, and the few white clouds had cleared into a deep blue sky as I drove along a narrow hedgerow lane. Two wooden poles propped the Skegness Grammar School gates wide open. A little circular drive led to the main building. The school was a Victorian structure, rendered in red brick that the salt air had turned pale. Turrets and criss-cross lattice windows adorned the front. Some thirty yards of neat green lawn separated the building from a modern, low, concrete, flat-roofed sports facility beyond which were tennis courts and fields for rugby, football, cricket, and half a dozen other sports.

I parked in a visitor space, climbed out of the car, mentally went over the list of questions I'd already written on a notepad, and breathed deep the fresh salt air. The sound of the sea crashing on the beach was audible above the shouts of teenagers playing on a distant field.

I strolled along a gravel path into the cool, dim lobby where a round, plump woman in her early sixties, with salt-and-pepper hair sat behind an enormous mahogany reception desk.

The woman said, "Can I help you?"

"Mrs Doris Cudlow. I'm here for an eleven a.m. meeting with the head librarian." I handed her my photo identification.

"Oh yes, we spoke earlier. Your appointment is all taken care of." The woman stood, gave a little friendly wave of the hand and said, "The librarian is waiting. Please follow me."

After a short walk along a wide hallway, we turned into a room with huge windows that overlooked the sports fields. Rows of tablet computers rested in docking stations, and a single cluster of bookshelves lined part of a far wall.

"Is this the library?" I asked, wondering about the lack of books.

"Oh yes, nice, isn't it? Everything is digital these days. We don't keep many physical items anymore." She pointed to the shelves of books. "Only local history material. When we get the funding, we'll digitise those as well."

We stopped, and she pointed at the glass door to an office that reminded me of a fish tank. "Please knock and enter. I've got to go back to reception."

Inside, a twentysomething woman, her face staring down into a computer screen, typed into a keyboard. She looked up when I tapped on the glass and waved me into the room.

"Layla Wilson," she said, extending her hand. "You must be my eleven o'clock—Mrs Cudlow?"

"That's right." I hesitated then smiled. "I was hoping to meet with the head librarian?"

Layla tilted her head back to the computer screen, and I thought she was going to sit down and send an e-mail requesting Emily Johnson join us. Instead, she said, "Oh, I'm new, and yes I'm the head librarian."

For a full three seconds, I stood there, stupefied, while the smile on my face faded. "Oh dear," I said at last then gave an uneasy little laugh. "I was hoping to speak with Emily Johnson."

Layla frowned. "Emily retired last month, not that it makes much difference. Everyone in town still thinks she works here. I can't tell you how many times parents come in and ask to speak with her directly, rather than myself."

She sat down with a thump and turned towards me, the glow from the computer screen fell full on her face, and I saw the look of disappointment in her eyes.

"Oh, I'm sorry," I said in a tone I hoped expressed regret at my mistake. "Local folk will soon get used to you; just hang on in there. It is only a matter of time. Did you say Emily left last month?"

"Officially, yes, but over the past few years Emily only worked a few months a year at the school, had a place in Wales. That's where she spent most of her time. With the digitisation of our collection over the past year, she decided it was time to step aside and let in new blood. Maybe I can help you?"

Already I could feel a sense of disillusionment gathering pace. I should never have driven out here, should have stayed in bed. Layla was new to the school; how could she help? I smiled, made an understanding noise but then decided it was worth explaining the reason for my visit. "I'm writing an article for the *Lincolnshire Weekly News* and was hoping to pick Emily's brain on a matter of local history. Have you heard of Fiona Fenchurch?"

"Who hasn't? She's the poor woman at the centre of the Dancing Hands Mystery."

"I'm trying to find out a little more about Fiona; that's why I wanted to chat with Emily. I hear she is the go-to person for local history."

Layla sighed. "Oh dear, I wish I could help, but I've only lived in town for a few months. I got this job straight out of university, graduate school."

I set my teeth into a smile to hide my disappointment; another wasted morning. "Well, it was worth a try."

Layla glanced at her watch. "Why don't you join me for lunch; we have to take it early before the kids."

I was about to reject the idea when she said, "My treat."

When you are flat broke, a free meal can't be sniffed at. "Well, I haven't eaten yet today..."

Layla flashed a friendly smile. "One of the older ladies will join us. I'm sure she will tell you everything you want to know about Fiona Fenchurch."

Chapter 61

WE SAT AROUND A TABLE in a small, box-shaped, gunmetal-grey cafeteria, with the smell of boiled vegetables mixed with scents of stewed meat and the distinct tang of fresh paint.

"At least they've coated the walls. Not sure about the colour, but it's better than the mottled splotches we had to endure yesterday," said Layla. "Shepherd's pie with boiled cabbage and blancmange for dessert. It's the same every Thursday."

I stared down at my oversized plate. A greyish gravy oozed from under lumpy mashed potatoes. "Exactly as I remember school dinners. Here goes," I said, taking a bite. I chewed vigorously for a moment. "Umm... mystery meat?"

Layla laughed. "Yep, could be beef, could be pork."

"Nope, you're wrong about that. It is squirrel meat," said a woman pulling up a chair. "Cheryl Moore, by the way." It was the receptionist I'd met earlier.

"Doris Cudlow," I said, waving a lumpy fork of mashed goo in acknowledgement.

Layla said, "Cheryl is the most efficient receptionist cum administrator, come-do-anything-you-need person in the world."

"Compliments will get you everywhere. You know that, don't you?" Cheryl scooped up a forkful of shepherd's pie, stared at it for a moment, then popped it into her mouth. When she finished chewing she said, "They should pay us danger money for this."

"It was worse in my day," I said. "Back then, the kitchens were next to the classrooms. We always knew what hellish concoction was coming way before lunchtime. Everyone cried on Tuesdays, even the teachers—liver and onions!"

Cheryl laughed. "Poor lamb!"

We fell into silence as we poked and prodded the lumps of glutinous goo on our plates. There was a pleasant comradery as we chewed and digested. When it was over, Layla put down her fork and said, "I'll get the dessert. Back in a few minutes. Oh, and Doris is researching Fiona Fenchurch."

Cheryl glanced at me with an expression I couldn't read. "Is that so?"

I watched Layla wander over to the food counter and said, "Yep, I thought I'd do a little digging into Fiona's disappearance."

Cheryl folded her arms. "Why the interest?"

I could tell by the look in her eyes she was sizing me up. "I'm a reporter—"

"No, thank you!" Cheryl's lips solidified into a straight line. "We've had enough salacious gossip about poor Fiona... and to think the police haven't caught her killer. After the latest fiasco, I doubt they ever will. Poor Fiona. I think it is about time we let sleeping dogs lie."

As I sat there digesting her words, it struck me hard and for the first time that Fiona Fenchurch was once an actual person. Until now, I'd seen her only as a desiccated skeleton covered in ragged clothes. But she'd lived and breathed as I did. The only difference that a tragic circumstance cut her life short. It wasn't fair. I said, "I hope she gets justice. Maybe the current interest by the news media will uncover a clue."

Cheryl grunted. "Bloody press are always sensationalising things."

"You knew Fiona, then?" I touched my handbag, ready to take out my notebook.

"There is nothing I can tell you."

I tried to keep my expression blank, but disappointment crept into my voice. "That's a shame. You see, I worked at the museum as a part-time security guard. It was I who found Fiona's body. I want to find out a little about the woman, for closure. Later, I'll write an article. It won't be sensationalistic; I can assure you of that."

Cheryl opened her mouth then closed it and stared hard into my face. "You found Fiona's body?"

"Yes."

"And work security for the Beachside Museum?"

"That's right."

"Is Captain Honeybush still head of security?"

"Yep."

There was an intensity in Cheryl's eyes that left me unsettled. "How long have you been working for him?"

"Only a few days. I found Fiona's body on my first night."

Cheryl touched my arm. "Try to find another job, and whatever you do, keep away from the captain."

That I already knew but said, "Why?"

Cheryl pursed her lips. "Doris, I used to work at the museum. Loved the job because it gave me a little extra money. I worked the night shift at the weekend. If it weren't for Captain Honeybush, I'd still be there. Stay away from the man. He's creepy."

I slipped a hand into my handbag, pulled out my notebook and pen, and said, "Did you complain about the captain?"

"To who? He's in with the board members. They don't listen to part-time security guards. If you speak up the captain will crush you. He has a furious temper. It's a wonder he hasn't killed anyone."

I thought about that and said, "Maybe if enough people complain, something would be done about the man."

Cheryl gazed into my eyes as if scanning my inner thoughts. "So, he's been creepy with you, eh?"

Before I answered, she picked up a fork, leaned across the table, and with eyes blazing said, "What did you do about it, eh? Who did you complain to?"

Stunned, I slumped back in my chair. I hadn't complained to anyone, hadn't even said a word to Grace Rivers, yet. "Err... well—"

Cheryl dropped the fork. It clattered and rolled, scuttering to a stop on my side of the table, its prongs pointed at me. "This is a small town. People talk, and gossip spreads like wildfire. It is easier to walk away, especially if you want another local job."

"Desserts' up," said Layla, returning to the table with a tray and three dessert bowls. "Strawberry blancmange all round!"

The conversation ceased, and for several minutes we each chased the slippery dessert around our plates.

"Haven't tasted this in years," I said, devouring the last slither. "Can't say I miss it, but it brings back memories."

"Talking of memories, you asked about Fiona Fenchurch?" Cheryl placed her hands on the table. "What is it you want to know?"

"Anything you remember." I pulled out my notebook. "What can you tell me about her?"

"Fiona worked at this school as the assistant librarian." Cheryl turned to Layla. "Way before your time. By all accounts, she was a hard worker, never late, saved her pennies, and got on well with everyone."

I said, "Anything else?"

Cheryl closed her eyes. "Fiona also worked for a while as a part-time security guard at the Beachside Museum."

I scribbled in my notebook and said, "The overnight shift?"

Cheryl slowly opened her eyes and toyed with her dessert spoon. Clearly, she was considering her words. "From what I hear she didn't stay long... Captain Honeybush."

I looked at Cheryl thoughtfully. "When did you first meet Fiona?"

"Oh, me? Never. Fiona left the grammar school before my time."

I put down the pen and stared hard. "You never met Fiona Fenchurch?"

Cheryl shook her head. "I only knew about her through Emily Johnson, and only then because of the Dancing Hands Mystery. If you want more details, why don't you drive over to Monksthrope? Emily has an apartment in the Monksthrope Retirement Community."

Chapter 62

WHEN I GET CURIOUS about something, I often become like a bloodhound on a scent. Fiona Fenchurch was a mystery, and I wanted to find out more about her. Yes, there was the *Lincolnshire Weekly News* article, but more than that there was the woman herself and a growing sense of injustice at her unsolved murder. That's why I drove the ten miles to Monksthrope.

The retirement community sat atop a hill with views down into a green valley. A random cluster of single-level houses surrounded a larger building. Neatly trimmed lawns edged up to an enormous rockery; in the distance an orchard of fruit trees swayed in the gentle breeze, their tiny blossoms dotting white splotches on the green landscape. Everywhere pink and red peonies bloomed.

For a while, I sat in the car and gazed out of the windows. The happy shouts of children mingled with the occasional bark of a dog. An elderly lady in a bright summer dress walked a cat on a lead. Monksthrope Retirement Community wasn't the dingy, dark, depressing, old-people's home I remembered as a child. Sure, there were more elderly people picking their way through the grounds with walking sticks than you'd see on a regular street. But even from the car, I sensed an upbeat mood about the place.

I braced myself to quiz Emily Johnson about the Dancing Hands Mystery, stepped out of the car, and walked with determined steps towards the main building.

Inside, the receptionist said, "Emily Johnson?" She glanced up at a clock on the wall. "Emily will be in her Zumba class right now. That's in the gym, along the hall and to your left, but you'll need to be quick. The class is almost over."

I hurried along the hallway, almost running into a young boy.

"Watch out! You're not supposed to run in here." He pointed at a sign in supersized letters.

NO RUNNING IN THE HALLWAY – APPLIES TO RESIDENTS AND GUESTS.

I said, "Don't know if you'd call a fast walk a run, but I guess I ought to slow down a little." It was then I recognised his scowling face. "Tommy Peachtree?"

"Yeah," he said. "That's me."

Thinking back a few days to my stroll on the beach, I said, "Tommy, I helped you build a sandcastle. Do you remember?"

"Yeah, and only because you smashed my model of Tattershall Castle!" He paused, remembered his manners and said, "Thank you for all your help."

"Ah," I said, leaning forward. "I also saw you in the museum, at the I.A. Channer exhibition."

"You did?" he asked, voice excited. "Did you like my spooky dance moves?"

"Tommy's been practising at the Monksthrope Little Thespian Club class all week," said a familiar female voice.

I turned around to see his mother, Ruby Peachtree. She said, "They even shot a video of him being chased away by Mr Channer."

Tommy said, "I had to ask for an autograph and run away as Mr Channer threw sand at me."

Ruby said, "It's supposed to be an art exhibit called *Artist Gets Mad At Success*. It will screen at the end of the exhibition along with Mr Channer's *Drunk Man on Bench*."

"Ahh," I said, face flushing. "Isn't that wonderful."

Ruby nodded. "Tommy has another live *Spook 'Em* performance with the other actors tonight. The museum has shifted their hours and don't open until nine thirty."

"Late night for Tommy, eh?"

"That's right," replied Ruby, offering a hand to shake and a smile. "And the crowd will be even bigger!"

"Good for you, Tommy," I said, ruffling the boy's hair with a hand.

Ruby said, "Do you have a relative living in the retirement community as well?"

"No, just hoping to speak with a resident."

"It's a great facility. I've made so many older friends." Ruby scratched her chin thoughtfully. "Who are you looking for?"

"Emily Johnson."

"That's Grandma," cried Tommy. "She's dancing in the gym. Follow me."

Chapter 63

RUBY, TOMMY, AND I waited outside the glass doors of the gymnasium. It did little to drown out the upbeat tempo as the residents moved and shuffled with amazing synchronicity. With the practised eye of a journalist, I scanned the crowd for Emily Johnson. She was near the front of the class, in a black-and-yellow-tiger leotard, and kept up, step for step, with the instructor.

"Impressive," I said as I thought about Mrs Lintott's suggestion I join a gym. "Doubt if I could have kept up with your mother when I was in my twenties: no chance now."

"Mum turned eighty this year. She's been into fitness since she bought a little caravan in Wales," said Ruby. "That's why she loves it in this community. I grew up around these parts in Anderby, not too far from here. My husband works in Coventry, so we moved away."

The music stopped. A low murmur of conversation carried out through the glass doors. As the instructor fiddled with the electronic equipment, I saw him—Mr Christy. His oversized hands rested on his hips as he leaned forward to catch his breath.

I'd seen him with Tommy in the Beachside Museum and wondered about the connection. I pointed and said, "Do you know that man?"

Ruby smiled then said, "Oh, that's Peter, Mum's boyfriend. He's a retired accountant, good with numbers. Makes things too, woodwork. Very good with his hands."

A new tune played over the speakers. I recognised its opening notes. The same song played when I "danced" barefoot on the beach with Mr Christy. Automatically, my hand flew to my throat.

I watched with a growing fascination as the instructor turned to the class and shuffled back and forth, arms outstretched like a zombie. Mr Christy hurried to the front of the class. His gigantic hands rose to throat level, fingers opening and closing like the pincers of a giant crab. Then he shuffled forward, advancing on the instructor. The whole thing was like a scene from a 1980s B-rated horror movie. Everyone in the room had their arms outstretched, fingers opening and closing—an army of Monksthrope zombies on the march.

"That's the latest dance craze to sweep the retirement community," Ruby muttered as she and Tommy joined in. "Last year it was the Walking Stick Pogo."

"Oh, I see," I said, removing my hand from my throat. "Seems I missed out on that spooky dance craze."

Another song began, with a frenetic beat. Everyone waved their arms in the air and swayed from side to side like trees in the sea breeze.

The instructor yelled, "Boop-ya-wee-boo-ya-wee!"

"Wee-wee-wee!" yelled the class.

I turned to Ruby. "Another dance craze?"

She nodded and said, "Tell you what, you'll get more sense out of Mum when she has had a little rest. After class, she likes to have a shower and change into her afternoon clothes. Give me your phone number; I'll let her know you are here, and you two can meet in the rockery, say in forty-five minutes?"

Chapter 64

A BLAZING SUN SHONE in a cloudless, blue sky. An eastern breeze carried the scents from the sea, and birdsong filled the soft salt air. A lovely afternoon to relax and chat. I sat with Emily Johnson on a wooden bench in the rockery under the leafy shade of a massive oak tree, looking out onto row upon row of red-and-pink mottled peonies.

"Doris Cudlow, you say." Emily studied my face then her sharp eyes closed. After a moment, her entire body gave a curious little quiver and became very still. Except for her eyeballs, which under closed lids, appeared to dart this way and that as if in search of a lost memory.

After a full ten seconds, I said, "Are you quite all right?"

Her eyes snapped open. She smiled. "Very well, thank you. Just practising a yoga memory recall technique I learned in a commune in Wales."

"Oh, I see."

"Have you been to Wales?" Her eyes never left my face as she spoke, darting back and forth like an image scanner at the Skegness General Hospital.

"Oh yes, loved it, especially the mountains," I said, just a little unnerved, then added, "Where was your commune?"

"Perlysiau Village, just outside of Bargoed, small town, quaint." Emily's sharp eyes rolled over the length of my body. "Perhaps a little too 1960s hippy for you, though." Again, she closed her eyes, and her body seemed to quiver, became still, and sank into a deep tranquillity.

I leaned forward, watching Emily's yogic memory-recall practice with a mixture of fascination and concern. Although eighty, she could pass for a woman in her late fifties. After a full thirty seconds, her eyes snapped open. "Can't recall a Cudlow in these parts. Not local, are you?"

"No. Not local." As the words came out, I wondered if Emily had a photographic memory for names. "I moved down from London not too long ago. I don't suppose you know Whispering Towers Boarding House?"

Her answer was immediate. "Mrs Lintott's place?"

"That's right. I've lived there since I moved to town."

"Haven't seen her for a couple of years, at least. How is that cat of hers—Mr Felix?"

The woman had a fantastic memory. My hopes soared. It wouldn't be long before I knew all there was to know about Fiona Fenchurch and the circumstances of her disappearance. I said, "Both Mrs Lintott and the cat are very well."

Mentally I ran over the questions I'd jotted in my notebook and placed a hand on my bag, ready to pull it out if my memory faltered. At that precise moment, a seed of concern came sneaking slowly into my mind. I had to be careful, not rush too fast, lest I blow my chance. With caution replacing my eager rush, I deployed the first technique from the Positive Outcomes journalism course: "Sugar Coating" and said, "Mrs Johnson—"

She raised a hand. "Emily, please."

"Emily, you have a remarkable memory."

"Photographic for faces, pretty decent for facts." Her reply was modest, almost matter of fact. "I've only lived in this retirement community for a short while and can name every resident and member of staff. I've recently retired from the grammar school, knew the name and face of every child. Loved working in the school library but needed a change. Now, what can I do for you, Mrs Cudlow?"

I liked her direct approach. There was no need to beat about the bush. "Fiona Fenchurch."

Her ancient neck turned in my direction, and her eyes narrowed a fraction. "Now why in the world would an out-of-towner come to visit an old lady like me to ask questions about Fiona Fenchurch?"

She didn't wait for an answer.

"Because they want to find out all the grimy gossip, so they can publicise it on one of those online magazines, no doubt. Mrs Cudlow, are you one of those filthy dogs who call themselves a reporter?"

"Well... I... err..."

"A reporter and from London, eh?" Emily said the sentence as if it were something obscene. "I've nothing to say." She shuffled to the edge of the seat and stood up. "Goodbye, Mrs Cudlow."

Chapter 65

"PLEASE, I'M NOT A FULL-time reporter," I said. It sounded desperate. It was. "I'm drafting an article for the *Lincolnshire Weekly News*. I'm not looking for salacious gossip."

Emily placed her hands on her hips. "Then what do you want?"

"To find out about Fiona Fenchurch. What was she like?"

"You are not going to write gossip?"

"No."

"Or portray the Retirees' Spring Festival in a bad light?"

"No."

"Promise?"

"Of course, I promise," I answered and meant it. "I just want to find out what Fiona was like as a person."

Emily went quiet.

I waited, watching this older woman with more energy than I could muster after a pot of black coffee. There was a vitality about her, a joy of life and all things living. Emily Johnson, I thought, was the kind of person who'd die bungee jumping when the time came, drop dead skydiving from an aeroplane, or while dancing too vigorously to the latest retiree dance craze. And at eighty she was as sharp as a tack.

Still, I watched and waited.

Emily's eyes closed as her jaw moved from side to side in a sort of chewing motion, and slowly, the corners of her mouth twitched, slightly at first, until they curved into a full-out smile. Then her eyelids lifted, and her eyes shone like a mirror reflecting a bright light.

"Very sweet," Emily said, her voice as soft as morning birdsong.

"Fiona?"

Emily sat down. "Yes, she was the sweetest person I'd ever worked with. A hard worker, conscientious, concerned for the environment and her fellow man. But very shy too."

"Shy?"

"Oh yes. She'd always disappear when a camera came out, even on school photograph day." Emily paused. "I don't have a single image of her in my collection. You see, as well as being shy, Fiona was a die-hard minimalist: *leave the earth as you find it* type of person."

"Anything else?"

Emily closed her eyes. They did their curious little dance under the eyelids. "We worked together for three or four years at the grammar school. It was a long time ago... must have been over twenty-five years by now. Fiona was as regular as clockwork, enjoyed dance, took acting classes, painted, but moved away from Skegness—financial problems. I know she went to Wales, Cardiff. But we lost touch."

Eager to hear more, I said, "You say you fell out of touch?"

"Yes. After Fiona left the grammar school, I didn't see her very often. Occasionally, she'd stop by the school for lunch, usually on Thursdays. Back then they served shepherd's pie with boiled cabbage and blancmange for dessert, minced kidneys with onion gravy on Tuesdays—horrible dish. Fiona said she missed the school dinners."

"Did she come back to town much?"

Mrs Johnson shook her head. "Not often. But when Fiona was in Skegness, she made a special point of stopping by the school to visit... always around lunchtimes, though."

I was about to open my handbag to pull out my notebook when Emily said, "The last time I saw Fiona was about two years before the Dancing Hands Mystery."

I sat up straight. "Two years before?"

"That's right, might have been three, certainly not more than that."

"So, she didn't visit the school the day she went missing?"

"Nope. That's the strange thing. As far as I can remember, it was the only time she came back to town without stopping by."

I said, "She might have forgotten."

Emily turned to look at me. "Not Fiona; she liked her school dinners. We always paid for her, and that means a lot when you are strapped for cash. Anyway, Skegness was a much smaller town back then, and as you'll find out soon enough, everyone knows everyone's business."

I thought about that then said, "What do you remember about Fiona's last visit?"

"She'd just taken a job in Cardiff; finances were always difficult. It paid enough to get by. I always thought she'd come back here one day to live. Alas, she returned, but not how I'd imagined it—as a skeleton hidden in a dust-filled corner of the Beachside Museum." A tear formed at the corner of Emily's eye and rolled slowly down her cheek.

A toddler ran along the path, their grandfather behind, puffing and panting.

"Good to see you having some fun, Mr Knipe," Emily said with a wave. "I'm going with my grandson to the Beachside Museum later tonight. He's in the performance. Enjoy the ride for as long as it lasts, and when it is over, jump off fast."

The old man waved back then hurried after the child.

When they had passed, I said, "What can you tell me about the Beachside Museum housekeeper, Old Betty?"

Emily lowered her eyes and said, "I think you mean Betty Foxley."

"Is that the ghost's real name?"

Emily nodded. "Everyone around these parts calls her Old Betty on account of the occasional sighting at the Beachside Museum. What would you like to know about her?"

There were so many questions written in my notebook and filed in my mind. I ignored them and said, "I've heard stories that Betty's ghost was involved in the Dancing Hands Mystery."

"Go on," Emily said, leaning forward. "What have you heard?"

I shrugged. "I don't know if I've got it totally right, but some say the noise from the Retirees' Spring Festival upset Old Betty, and she did away with Fiona Fenchurch to disrupt the party."

Emily rolled her eyes. "That old chestnut! Well, there isn't a shred of truth in it. Betty Foxley was as sweet as a sun-ripened peach. Yes, she was stooped and sinewy like an old oak tree, but she wouldn't hurt a fly—vegetarian. Very unusual for her day."

"Oh, I thought she was some vengeful spectre."

"Yes, that is a popular myth." Emily sighed. "But there is not a shred of truth in that story. It is a bit of mischievous gossip spread by an ex-military man who should know better."

I sat up straight. There was little doubt in my mind about the person's identity, but I wanted confirmation. "A military man, you say. Who?"

Emily shook her head. "Sorry, I spoke out of turn. I'll not say the name, as I don't know for a fact who started the vengeful-spectre myth. What I will say is everyone who knew Betty loved her. That's why she stayed on as housekeeper well into her retirement years. Whoever killed Fiona Fenchurch, it wasn't the ghost of Betty Foxley."

Chapter 66

I TURNED TO GLANCE at the peonies. A bumblebee hovered above the petals. It landed, did a little dance, then after a moment, took flight. I watched it until it disappeared out of sight. The mystery surrounding Fiona Fenchurch seemed to be getting more transparent, and now I could just make out the edge of the puzzle.

Emily said, "Please give my phone number to Mrs Lintott. I'd like to reconnect. Ask her to text me." She read out the number.

I entered it into my phone. "Will do."

Emily touched my arm. "Now, you didn't say what you do."

"I'm a reporter."

"Don't be silly. I mean for your regular job. If you board at Mrs Lintott's place, you are unemployed, underemployed, or retired. How is Mr Pandy, by the way?"

"Good as far as I can tell." I let out a long slow sigh. "I came to Skegness to get away from London. Things worked out for a while when I got a job at the *Skegness Telegraph*."

Emily said, with a rueful shake of the head, "I've always enjoyed the printed word. But I have an e-book reader now, got to move with the times. I feel so sad the *Telegraph* had to close."

"Me too." I took a deep breath. "I feel like I've been on skid row since the newspaper went under."

Again she touched my arm. "This, too, shall pass."

"Eh?"

"My first husband used to say that when we ran into difficulties. And let me tell you we bumped into them aplenty. What are you doing now?"

"Until a few days ago, I worked at Fantasy Gardens Arcade... in the kitchen."

Emily giggled. "For Mr Hornsby, eh? Don't tell me you were one of his illicit doughnut-making workers?"

I grinned. "Do you work for the police?"

"Too old!"

"Then I'm guilty. Doughnut frying helped pay the bills."

Emily laughed. It was a warbling birdlike sound. "So, how are you getting by?"

"It's tough, but I'm used to living close to the bone. I've just accepted a position at the Beachside Museum."

"Doing what?" The words came out sharp like the warning squawk of a sparrow on sighting a hawk.

"Security."

Emily sucked in a sharp breath. "With Captain Honeybush?"

The way she said the man's name sent a chill along my spine. "That's right. I'll be working as his assistant."

Emily lowered her voice. "I know I'm getting on a bit in years, but take my advice—quit. Captain Honeybush ought not to oversee that place. When he gets into one of his blind rages, I don't think even he knows what he is doing. But you know how it goes with the old boys' network, I suppose."

Chapter 67

THE DASHBOARD CLOCK read three forty as I pulled into the Fiddlers Bowl Café car park tucked into a side alley off Prince George Street. I chose a space near the rear and flipped off the engine. I was early for my afternoon meal with Jenny, which was good because I was still digesting the conversation with Emily Johnson.

"I need more time with that woman, have to visit again."

After winding down the window, I took out my notebook, re-read my notes, then picked up a pen and jotted down what I'd learned about Fiona Fenchurch.

Fact one: Fiona worked at the grammar school and is still remembered as a cheerful and diligent worker—that says a lot for her character. Everyone liked the woman.

Fact two: She also worked for a while as a part-time security guard at the Beachside Museum.

Fact three: She moved to Wales, found a respectable job, and came back to Skegness for infrequent visits. From what I'd learned, it seemed as if she was a woman who thrived on routine. One of which was a visit to the grammar school, but she hadn't done that on her last visit—why?

Fact four: The case sits in the unsolved file at the Skegness police station. Given the recent publicity, they appear to be in no hurry to bring Fiona's disappearance back into the spotlight.

Fact five: The source of the tale about Old Betty dragging Fiona into the sea came from Captain Honeybush.

"Or at least," I said aloud, "that is what I take from Emily Johnson's comments."

I mulled that over, wrote "Captain Honeybush" on an empty page, circled it, and stared hard at the letters until my eyes bugged out. Then I chewed the end of the pen and considered what to do next.

The phone rang, and I jerked in surprise, not expecting a call. Glancing at the screen didn't help; I didn't recognise the number.

"Doris Cudlow, how can I help you?"

"This is Ruby Peachtree. We spoke earlier at the Monksthrope Retirement Community." A breathlessness in her voice made me think the worst.

"It's your mother, isn't it?"

"Yes," she said, her breathing laboured and heavy.

I pressed the phone hard to my ear and sucked in a breath. "What's happened?"

Ruby didn't speak for several seconds, the sound of heavy gasps clearly audible. "Sorry about that," she said at last. "Mum had me join her afternoon jog team. It's no fun when you are outrun by a bunch of octogenarians!"

I let out a breath, long and slow. "So, everything is all right, then?"

"Oh yes, Mum told me she forgot to mention something to you earlier."

"What?"

"I'm not sure if it is important, but she remembered Fiona had a good friend she'd often talk about. Mum never met her, so I guess that is why she forgot."

That surprised me. "A boyfriend?"

"No, a woman friend. I believe her name is Jenny Styles."

Chapter 68

I ENTERED THE FIDDLERS Bowl Café a little after four: a mixture of locals and tourists hunched over plastic tables with red-white-and-blue-faded tablecloths. The air was thick with the savoury aromas of dinner, and a dozen excited conversations discussed the evening's upcoming I.A. Channer exhibition.

Jenny sat at a window table, plum beret perched at an angle with rebellious strands of hair sticking out as she peered through her reading glasses at the menu. "Hullo, honey. Looks like they've got some new dishes for us to enjoy."

I slipped into a seat opposite, nodded at the waitress for a pot of tea, and glanced at the menu. There was only one question on my mind, but it could wait. "Sorry I'm late. I had to take a call."

Jenny must have picked up on the tension in my voice. She glanced up, twiddled with the gold chain attached to her glasses, and said, "Honey, what's wrong?"

I said, "Jenny, I'm trying to find out as much as possible about Fiona Fenchurch."

A warm smile filled her face. "That would be lovely. So often we forget the dead."

The waitress placed a pot of tea on the table. "Back in a moment to take your orders."

When the waitress left, Jenny said, "Doris, I'd like to help. What information are you looking for?"

I poured, added milk and sugar, and said, "Anything about her life—friends, photos, letters, stuff like that. As you know, I'm pulling together an article for the *Lincolnshire Weekly News*."

Jenny took off her reading glasses and said, "I thought that was about Old Betty and her life as the museum housekeeper?"

"It is, but I also need to dig a little into the life of Fiona Fenchurch."

The waitress appeared. "Today's special is shepherd's pie with rhubarb blancmange for dessert."

"Treat's on me," said Jenny. "We'll take the special twice and another pot of tea."

The waitress jotted down the order. "If you need anything else, holler."

I blew on the surface of my cup and took a sip. "What can you tell me about Fiona?"

A sharp change came over Jenny. Tears rolled down her cheeks as her face reddened. "Oh, honey, it was terrible."

Alarmed at the sudden change, I said, "What happened?"

Jenny picked up a paper napkin and dabbed her eyes. "It is all too much for me." Her voice was barely a whisper. "Just too much."

"I'm listening, Jenny."

"The Beachside Museum has taken everything. Same with the hospice. I can't do it anymore. I'm drained. If it weren't for my little breaks in France, I'd be six feet under. And now with Fiona's body showing up..."

I said, "Tell me about Fiona."

"There is nothing to tell. Nothing I haven't already told the police."

My voice softened. "I'd like to hear all about it, anyway."

Jenny shot me a look out of the corner of her eye, inhaled, and let out a slow breath. "This is not something I talk about much. I can't sleep most nights, won't tonight, given what I will tell you."

"Go on, please."

Jenny gazed at me with concern, her hands resting on the table. Then her eyes drifted away to look out of the window. "Fiona Fenchurch was the best friend I've ever had."

"You two were friends?" I tried to sound surprised, but may have overdone it.

Jenny stared at me for a long moment then said, "I suppose you already knew that."

I said, "What was she like?"

"There was no one like her in the entire world. She was sweet, easy to get on with, and very generous."

I said, "That's what I've heard."

Jenny raised a plump hand, her round hazel eyes wide. "No, no, you don't understand. Words don't do Fiona justice. She was honest, overflowed with integrity, loyal to the last, and served her community."

Everyone I'd met liked Fiona Fenchurch, but Jenny's rant was just too much. "Come on, no one is that perfect."

I was shocked when, after only the briefest pause, Jenny's voice became a high-pitched shrill. "Oh, honey, Fiona was shy, a minimalist. She never got angry, never a word out of place, always there when I needed help. Do you see? Fiona Fenchurch was like an angel!"

I eased off on my cynicism and said. "Yes, I'm getting the picture."

Jenny's hands covered her eyes for an instant, and she let out a bitter laugh—a hollow, soulless sound. Then she spoke as if to herself. "Fiona was always there for me. And the one day I should have been at her side, I wasn't."

"The day she disappeared?" I said, seeking clarity.

Jenny's eyes narrowed as she recalled the details. "I was out of town that day. If I'd had been on the beach, Fiona might never have vanished. Don't you see? It is all my fault. I don't even have any photographs of her. I can't sleep at night for thinking about what happened. That's why I volunteer for the overnight shift at the hospice. I might as well do some good rather than toss and turn in bed."

"Oh, Jenny," I said and held her hand. "The past few years must have been tough."

She stared at me with tear-stained cheeks. "Do you know Fiona worked at the Beachside Museum as a security guard, overnight shift? It was only for a short while because of..." Again she broke out into a sob.

"Go on," I said in a soft voice, eager to hear it all.

In between sobs, Jenny said, "That's why when there are female security guards on duty, I volunteer the overnight shift too."

"I see," I said, and I did. Everything was becoming very clear.

Jenny said, "I've had enough of that bloody, awful museum. I was there earlier. Do you know Alicia Osborn, the new security guard?"

"We've met."

Jenny folded her arms. "Alicia sought me out, her eyes wide as if she'd seen too much—Captain Honeybush."

I said, "That man is... creepy."

"We really ought to do something." Jenny's voice was low and severe. "Doris, has the man been creepy with you? Tell the truth; you are amongst friends."

Chapter 69

AFTER I LEFT THE FIDDLERS Bowl Café, the conversation with Jenny continued to tumble around in my mind. It was time to do something about Captain Honeybush, find evidence to back up my suspicions, and lance the boil. With no desire to return to the archives section of the Beachside Museum, I drove the short distance to the Skegness Central Library.

Inside the modern concrete-and-glass structure, I hurried by the reception desk, next to which was a sign:

Toilets to your left.

Meeting point for lost kids is at the children's library check-out desk.

Hours 9 a.m. to 6:30 p.m. Monday – Friday.

Closed Saturday during Retirees' Spring Festival.

Closed Sunday.

I searched amongst the books, magazines, newspapers, and through dusty boxes. Anything to do with the *Dancing Hands Mystery* I tossed onto my "to read" pile. Soon, I'd gathered a sizable collection of material.

Seated at a table in a quiet corner, I read. The articles only confirmed what I already knew. There was only vague information about Fiona Fenchurch, unconfirmed reports about the events that day on the beach, but no new information—no fresh insight. After an hour, my lack of progress left me frustrated. My enthusiasm ebbed, and with the clock counting down until my first shift at the museum on Friday, I was desperate.

Something tapped my shoulder. I turned around.

There was no one there.

The tap came again.

I looked down.

A girl, no older than five with round, brown eyes and two ponytails tied with pink ribbons, smiled back. In her hand she carried a small leather-bound journal. She said, "Are you a movie star?"

"Me? No, I'm a... journalist."

"What's that?"

I pointed at the pile of the table. "A writer."

"Oh! You look like one of those people from the movies. Can I have your autograph?" She placed her journal on the table.

"Sure," I said, signing the blank page with a flourish.

"Thank you."

I glanced around, didn't see her parents. "Where is your mum?"

"Not here."

"Oh, so you came with your dad?"

"Yes."

Again, I glanced around. There was no sign of a distraught parent.

I said, "Where is he?"

"He got lost." She turned to point at the rows of shelves. "In the book forest."

"Ah! Let's take you to the children's library reception desk. I'm sure your dad will be there."

And sure enough, he was.

"Thank you," he said, giving his daughter a hug.

The girl said, "Daddy. That lady is a famous writer, and I got her autograph!"

I shrugged, gave a little wave, and went back to my research.

After another hour of fruitless reading, I sank back in my chair in frustration and pushed the pile of documents to one side. Fatigue pressed down on my limbs. It felt like I was digging in clay. I glanced across the table long enough to notice that the person seated opposite had his head half-hidden in an oversized book on the history of Second World War military machines. I allowed my eyes to wander over the front and back cover, taking in the details of aeroplanes, tanks, and warships. The hand-drawn images were of high quality but were hardly relevant to the Dancing Hands Mystery.

Then when I least expected it, as the individual put the book down, an idea jumped into my mind. With quick steps, I headed to the history section, carefully selected a stack of books, and back at the table, scoured the contents. As I scanned the text, flipping the pages with a light hand, I suddenly paused. I re-read the section then again, this time writing with speed into my notebook. Finished, I pulled up my phone and did an internet search. It wasn't long until I found what I wanted. Finally, I got to my feet, let out a low whistle, hurried out of the library, sat in my car, and called Jenny Styles.

"Jenny, it's Doris... Okay... Okay... Yes, I'm with you... This evening at the museum, yes... What time? Eight? Okay, see you later."

There were other calls to make, things to line up. With speed, I went to work. It wasn't until almost 7 p.m. that I had everything in place.

Chapter 70

MY HEAD THROBBED AS I pulled my car into a parking space near the front of the Beachside Museum. I took two painkillers, swallowed, and stared at the historic Victorian building. Beyond the entrance, the sun sank westward, as a bank of dark clouds drifted low in the heavens. As I watched the dusk sky slowly darken, a cloudburst spewed down large raindrops.

The mini heatwave had broken.

The splotches soon turned into a hard grey rain that fell in great sheets like a dark curtain drawn across a London stage.

"It, too, shall pass," I said out loud. But, in truth, the wait churned up my nerves, and for a brief instant, I wondered whether I could go through with my plan. But I had all I needed to put Fiona Fenchurch's memory to rest.

There was no way back.

The wind worked up into a brief squall. Another burst of raindrops slapped against the car. They clattered and splashed on the windscreen, drummed on the roof, and rattled the door.

I rummaged around in my handbag for my mobile phone. I pressed the ON switch and stared at the screen saver. Mark Twain's quote flickered across the screen:

"Do the thing you fear most and the death of fear is certain."

A blinding burst of lightening shot across the darkened sky. I gasped, held tight on to the phone, and crouched low in the car seat as thunder crackled in the night air. As the rumble drifted off into the distance, I stared at the electronic device and the flickering letters, and I tried very hard to muster the courage to continue.

After a long slow breath, I punched numbers into the phone and said, "Hello, is this Captain Honeybush?"

"Indeed it is, and whom do I have the pleasure?" He slurred his words as he spoke.

I pressed the phone to my ear, blocking out the rain beating on the car, and said, "Doris Cudlow. Can we talk?"

"Why, Old Gal, you know the captain is always eager to pass the time of day with you." He paused, his voice replaced by a rustling sound. "I don't think I have you down to work this evening. You begin full-time tomorrow."

"That's right." I swallowed hard, my heart a steady thump against my chest. "But I'm at the museum now. I need to speak with you about a matter of some urgency."

A hint of caution entered his voice. "Really, Old Gal? Nothing official, I take it?"

"A rather personal matter of some importance to us both."

"Ah ha! Let's not go over this on the phone, never know who might be listening in, do you? How about I take you for dinner Friday after work, and after, the captain will show you around his command headquarters—a little bachelor pad off Dutton Avenue?"

I gagged at the thought but said, "Captain, this can't wait."

"I see. Don't like to mix business with pleasure, but at times it is a necessary part of the job. How about you come to my office?"

"If you are sure." I knew I was taking a big risk, one that could go terribly wrong. But during the meeting I'd stay near a door or an open window. That way I'd be able to make a quick escape.

"Oh wonderful," he said in a drunken slur. "See you in ten minutes, Old Gal."

I put the phone down, my heartbeat matching the pitter-patter pulse of the rain. Fast. Hard. Loud. If my plan failed, I'd look like a fool, and worse, an angry mob would drive me out of town headed by Captain Honeybush.

The rain eased.

A weak streak of yellow sunset illuminated the entrance to the museum. The only thing on my mind as I stepped out of the car was doing the right thing for Fiona Fenchurch and seeing justice run its course.

Chapter 71

FACE SET AND STERN, I strode into the lobby of the museum. Alicia Osborn sat behind the reception desk, a resigned smile on her face. She waved me over and called out.

"Doris, can I speak with you for a moment?"

I waved back, didn't speak, and kept moving. Now wasn't the time for conversation. Now was the time for action. When you are on an uncertain mission, forward momentum is your friend. If I didn't keep my legs moving towards Captain Honeybush's office, I knew they would turn and flee.

I marched down several flights of stairs, into a gloomy basement, and along a narrow, windowless passageway, all the while clutching my handbag tight. At last, I stood outside a solid-oak-panelled door. Attached at the top was a large gold, metal plate with "Captain Honeybush" etched in black lettering.

"Like a rat's lair," I muttered as I raised my hand to knock. Then a thought struck me.

It struck me hard like an object propelled with great force.

And it caused my hand to drop.

It was the realisation that deep down here in the basement, the captain's office had to be a windowless room.

There was only one way in, and one way out.

I hesitated a moment to reconsider my options.

The oak-panelled door flew open. A sour whiff of stale alcohol drifted into the hallway.

"Mrs Cudlow, Old Gal. What a pleasant surprise." The captain stared from his beady, brown eyes—two peanuts set in a mound of risen bread dough. His fat fingers clasped tight around a crystal tumbler. The yellow liquid inside sloshed. "Come on inside."

Too late, Doris, I told myself as I stepped over the threshold, got to go with the original plan.

The captain waited by the doorway until I was inside his office. Then with a flourish, he closed the door. It snapped shut with a solid click.

The room was large, panelled, with potted plants in the corners and oversized prints of thoroughbred racehorses in full gallop on the walls.

"Take a seat, Old Gal." His brown eyes twinkled. "How about a little something to help you relax: brandy or gin?"

I glanced around the windowless room. It was neat, tidy, with everything in its place. I calculated it would take less than ten seconds for me to run and escape out into the hallway. Only then did I take a seat at his huge mahogany desk, my back to the door. "Brandy and soda water, if you have any."

"Ah, very well, Old Gal." The captain lumbered drunkenly to a little side table at the far side of his room. Various half-empty glass bottles clustered together like shoppers in a market—whiskey, brandy, gin, stood side by side with a large ice bucket and a soda maker.

After several moments he returned with the drink.

"There you go, Old Gal." The captain leaned in close as he spoke. Too close.

With a hand I willed not to shake, I took the glass. "Cheers," I said, putting it to my lips but not swallowing.

The captain's eyes gleamed like an adventurer uncovering a vast treasure. "Bottoms up, Old Gal." He lifted his glass and downed half the contents. "That's better, isn't it?"

I placed the glass on the desk and said, "Captain, there is something I'd like to—"

Without warning, he lurched forward, hands grasping at my body. I reared back, evading his initial lunge. Again he sprang forward, catching my left wrist between plump fingers. I knocked his hand away, twisted out of his grasp, and stumbled behind the desk.

This wasn't part of the plan.

He laughed with enthusiastic gusto as he lumbered to the side of the desk. "Tally-ho, Old Gal. The joy is in the chase, not the kill, don't you know. Tally-ho!"

I fumbled with my bag, pulled out my phone, pressed record, and shouted, "Captain Honeybush, you have rather a nasty reputation for abusing your female staff, don't you?"

His voice fell to an intoxicated growl. "Indeed, I do. Come here, Old Gal. Ha-ha-ha." He scrambled around the desk. "Captain's orders."

Once again, I evaded his drunken clutches. I waved the phone. "Stop right now!"

Captain Honeybush half turned, stumbled back a few steps, and reached for his cane.

"Tally-ho, Old Gal. Tally-ho!"

With an athletic movement, he swung the walking stick. It struck the phone. I watched with growing horror as it flew out of my grasp and landed on the opposite side of the desk, near the door.

"Capital shot, Mrs Cudlow, don't you think?"

I stared towards the door. Panic almost buckled my knees. The only way to get the phone was to get by the captain.

"Oh bugger!"

He smoothed down the corners of his waxy moustache with a thumb and forefinger then raised the cane above his head. A dark lizard like tongue darted out, circling his thick lips, and his brown eyes glittered with a devilish delight, as once again, he lumbered forward.

Chapter 72

A LIGHT TAP-TAP-TAP sounded on the door.

The captain stopped mid-stride then whirled around to face the entrance.

The door creaked open with a sharp squeal.

Alicia Osborn stepped into the office.

For one insane second the captain looked as if he'd attack. But he staggered back, lowered the cane, leaned an arm on his desk, and cursed, his voice breaking into a furious growl. "What the dickens is the meaning of this?"

I said, "Captain, Alicia is with me, that is what I was about to tell you before you attacked me."

"Mrs Cudlow," he began in his Oxbridge accent, all nasal and superior. "I did no such thing. Nothing but friends talking over a celebratory drink. Congratulations on joining my team. Now, Alicia, I'm sure whatever it is you want to speak with me about can wait. You can leave now."

I said, "Captain, Alicia isn't going anywhere. You've done enough damage. It is time for you to step down and go." As I spoke, I scrambled around the desk, stooped to pick up my phone, all the while my eyes never left his face.

Again, the office door opened. Jenny Styles hurried in, reading glasses swaying on a loose gold chain. "Sorry I'm late."

We formed a semicircle around the man.

Jenny raised a finger, pointed at the captain and said, "Doris is a reporter. She knows all about you and will make you pay for your crimes!"

The captain's doughy face went blank. "A reporter, are you, Mrs Cudlow?" There was a quiet calculation about his voice. "Well, then, you know you'll have to get your facts straight before spreading malicious gossip."

"I've got all the facts I need," I said.

His eyes narrowed to the cold, unreadable stare of a seasoned poker player. He jabbed a finger at Alicia, then Jenny, and finally me. "If you don't leave my office this instant, I'll see to it you never work here again or anywhere else in Skegness."

It didn't sound like a bluff.

No one spoke.

His words hung in the air for a full sixty seconds, then Alicia said, "Doris, perhaps this was a mistake."

Without making a sound, the captain slipped behind his desk, picked up the glass tumbler, and finished it with a satisfied glug. Then he looked at his watch. "Now, you have thirty seconds to get out."

Alicia moved to the door. I reached out an arm to hold her back and said, "Captain, we don't give up that easily. You might scare one of us, but together we will push back until you are behind bars."

He stood, fury bubbling up. "No one disobeys the orders of Captain Napoleon Honeybush. It'll be your word against mine. What evidence have you got, eh? Nothing!"

For a brief instant, the fear that weakened my legs and roiled my stomach gave way to anger. I held out my mobile phone and yelled, "Really? There is our earlier conversation, for a start."

Captain Honeybush lifted his chin towards the device, small eyes widening. "Why you filthy scoundrel!"

In a continuous movement, I turned up the volume and pressed play.

A low hiss sounded, followed by a crackle. Nothing else.

Beads of sweat rolled down my forehead stinging my eyes. I spun around to Alicia. In a panicked voice I said, "Did you get the cassette player?"

"Yes, it was in the desk drawer of the *Lincolnshire Weekly* archives reception area." Alicia lowered her eyes. "But the tape was blank."

Chapter 73

I GAZED AT ALICIA AS if her words had no meaning, but gradually my mind processed her sentence into reluctant, astonished acceptance. Then I drew in a nervous breath and said, "Blank?"

"I think we'd better go now," said Alicia in a mooselike whisper.

Jenny tugged at her reading glasses and said, "It's over, Doris." She turned to face the captain. "I'm done with this place. I quit as a volunteer. I'm done with this town too."

In a slow-motion movement, the captain sat down, placed his hands palms down on the desk, eyes glowing with victory, and in a low even voice said, "Now, everyone out of my office, except Mrs Cudlow."

Alicia shuffled towards the door, jumped back in astonishment as it opened before her hand reached the handle.

Captain Honeybush's eyes widened as Constable Wriggly strode into the room.

No one spoke.

The captain reached out a hand for his glass, swirled the remnants of ice. It tinkled softly like a distant bell. At last, with eyes narrowed and calculating, he said. "Why, Constable, what brings you here tonight?"

Before Constable Wriggly could speak, I squared my shoulders a little and stepped towards the desk. In a soft voice I said, "Albert, it is time to end this game."

The captain smoothed his moustache, tilted his head, eyes wide. "What did you say?"

"Albert Honeybush, grandson of Lieutenant Colonel George Honeybush of the Lancashire Fusiliers. That's you, isn't it?"

The captain stared but didn't speak, his plump lips a hard, straight line.

I said, "You never served in the army. How could you? The Lancashire Fusiliers ceased to exist in 1968. But your grandfather served in that regiment, in the battle of Gallipoli."

The captain stood up, breathing heavily, face purple with rage. "You devil!"

I took a step backwards and said, "Are you still blacklisted from membership of the pacifist party?"

His doughy mound of a face seemed to scrunch up. But now there was more fear than fury in his eyes. "How the hell did you find out about that?"

I said, "Sexual harassment, wasn't it?"

"That was over thirty years ago!"

Constable Wriggly said, "We better talk about this at the station. Now let's be having you, sir."

The captain's eyes darted madly about the room. In a continuous motion, he picked up his cane, and swinging it in a wide arc, lunged at the officer. For an instant, the two men struggled, twisting and turning, making it hard to see exactly what was happening, until it was too late. Constable Wriggly staggered back against the wall. The captain's cane connected with his head. The officer's knees gave way, and he crumpled slowly down to the floor.

Captain Honeybush fled.

Chapter 74

FOR A LONG MOMENT, a hushed silence fell over the room. Then all at once everyone spoke.

"Oh my God, he's dead," Jenny wailed. "Captain Honeybush killed him!"

"I'll call for an ambulance," Alicia said, jabbing at her phone.

"Wait! Let me check." I sent a text message then hurried forward, stooped down, and placed a hand at the side of the stricken officer's neck. A vigorous pulse pounded back.

Constable Wriggly moaned.

"Ease him up a little," Alicia said, taking the officer by his shoulder.

His eyes opened.

I leaned towards him and took his hand. "Can you hear me?"

He eased himself up a little further and sat still, blinking. "Think so. Give me a moment, and I'll be as right as rain."

"Shall I call for an ambulance?" Alicia knelt by the officer, her face ashen.

He held up a hand to indicate quiet. For several minutes he remained almost motionless. Only his eyes blinked like the cursor of a rebooting computer.

At last, Constable Wriggly rubbed the side of his head, staggered to his feet, and said, "I'm a little shaky, but I'll be fine."

Jenny said, "Captain Honeybush tried to kill you and ran off."

"Aye, that's right, lethal weapon, that cane of his nearly took my head off." The officer rubbed the back of his head, eyes darting around the office.

Jenny let out an anxious, little laugh. "Are you going to go after him?"

The constable hesitated for a moment then folded his arms. "No. I'll have to call this one in. The captain won't get far, though." He turned to face me and said, "Mrs Cudlow, thank you for calling me here to make the arrest. I only wish I knew where the killer was now—this is personal."

I turned to Jenny Styles and said, "Do you want to tell Constable Wriggly, or shall I?"

Jenny shot me a look out of the corner of her eye. "Tell the officer what exactly?"

"That you are Fiona Fenchurch."

She remained quite motionless, her eyes fixed on my face as though she'd not heard. "That's ridiculous!"

Constable Wriggly's eyes grew wide. He unfolded his arms.

"I think you will find," I said, turning to the officer, "the skeleton I found in the *Lincolnshire Weekly* archives is that of a Welsh woman—Miss Jenny Styles."

"What are you trying to say?" Jenny's voice was as cold and harsh as the north wind.

But I didn't have to say anything.

The office door squeaked open.

Emily Johnson stepped into the room. After a moment she said, "My God, Fiona, I thought you were dead!"

Chapter 75

THE FOLLOWING AFTERNOON at teatime...

"Another sausage roll, Constable?" said Mrs Lintott as she poured tea out of her "special occasion" china teapot. "Fresh today from Dee Dee's."

"Aye, that'd be lovely," said Constable Wriggly. "Can't beat the fresh-baked ones."

The three of us sat at Mrs Lintott's table enjoying an afternoon tea. Mr Felix watched, perched on the kitchen window ledge, eyeing the cream pot.

"Just popped by to give you an update," said the officer. He paused for a moment, took a greedy bite, and continued. "Fiona Fenchurch has made a full confession."

I said, "What did she say?"

Constable Wriggly spoke automatically as if reading from an official report. "Fiona Fenchurch befriended Miss Styles on a vacation to Wales. She moved out there to look for a job but continued to work the occasional weekend shift back here in Skegness at the Beachside Museum."

Mrs Lintott said, "Who was Miss Styles?"

"A retired schoolteacher, conservative sort, saved her pennies, never married, and retired on a state pension."

"Oh dear," said Mrs Lintott. "So, Fiona killed Miss Jenny Styles for her money and then took on the poor woman's identity?"

Constable Wriggly took a sip from his cup. "Seems so."

I said, "I hear Fiona was always short of cash. I suppose she saw in Jenny Styles an easy way to solve her financial problems."

Mrs Lintott picked up her cup and said, "But murder!"

The constable leaned back in his chair, slowly shaking his head from side to side. "Fiona said she didn't want to kill Miss Styles, but it was the only way to get her hands on the money. She used it for mini vacations to casinos in France."

"Dear God!" cried Mrs Lintott. "It's like something from one of those Hollywood movies. Who would have thought such a thing would happen in our little seaside town?"

For almost thirty seconds, there was only the tick-tock of the clock. Each of us, in our own way, trying to make sense of all that had unfolded.

I sighed, settled deep into my chair, toyed with the sausage roll on my plate. "At least the Dancing Hands Mystery has been solved."

Constable Wriggly shifted in his seat but only said, "Aye, that it has. A crafty trick it was too."

Mrs Lintott said, "Please explain."

I said, "Fiona was a seasoned thespian, amateur dramatics. She faked her collapse on the beach. Then in the chaos, simply got up and walked away."

"But how?" cried Mrs Lintott. "Constable Wriggly was there the entire time."

The officer lowered his eyes. "That's right, but..."

I said, "While he was being treated for sunstroke, Fiona saw her chance and slipped away. What with the music and dancing, she was unnoticed, as far as we can tell."

"But I thought Captain Honeybush helped," protested Mrs Lintott.

"That's right, he did," I said, "but the man was blind drunk. Isn't that so, Constable?"

The officer's head moved a fraction of a degree in agreement. "Not that you heard this from me, but that fact didn't make it into the official report." He paused as if a new understanding had popped into his mind. "I suppose that explains the captain's cock-and-bull story about Old Betty strangling the victim and dragging away the body into the sea."

I placed a hand on the side of my cheek. "I can't understand how the captain didn't spot the similarity between Fiona and Jenny. Do you suppose it was the alcohol that blinded him?"

The officer nodded. "And a little makeup, change of hair colour, different clothes, and the plum beret. That was enough to fool the captain, but not Emily Johnson."

"I wouldn't want to be in Captain Honeybush's shoes," said Mrs Lintott.

The officer said, "Constable Celia Bell arrested him at his apartment late last night. I wish I'd have been there." He rubbed the side of his head. "I suppose I must content myself in the fact that we'll throw the book at him; there'll be a slew of sexual harassment charges, and the Beachside Museum has ended his employment. He'll be in front of Judge Eboch."

Mrs Lintott glanced at Mr Felix, who sat motionless on the window ledge. "How did Fiona... do in Miss Styles?"

Constable Wriggly folded his arms. "Fiona encouraged Miss Styles to visit Skegness for the Retirees' Spring Festival. At the time Fiona worked the occasional weekend shift at the Beachside Museum. It was only natural for Miss Styles to visit her friend's place of work. They enjoyed a cup of tea together in the *Lincolnshire Weekly* archives reception area." He stared at his cup. "Tea laced with poison, Fiona dumped Miss Styles body in a disused storeroom. Rather than move the body, too heavy I suppose, she stayed on as a volunteer, and made sure no one ever entered the room."

"My God!" Mrs Lintott stared at the constable. "Fiona planned the wicked deed from start to finish."

"That's for the lawyers to argue about, I suppose." The officer lowered his voice. "Fiona's also under investigation for other frauds."

Mrs Lintott glanced at the kitchen door then back at the officer. "At the Beachside Museum?"

He placed his index finger on his lips. "At the hospice. There are some irregularities with former patients' finances. I can't say more than that just yet. But when the dust has settled, she'll be behind bars for a long time."

"Thank God!" said Mrs Lintott.

My mobile phone buzzed. I excused myself, stepped out into the hallway outside of Mrs Lintott's apartment. "Doris Cudlow, here."

The line crackled. "Can you hear me?"

"Yes, who is this?"

"Ah, that's better. Mrs Cudlow, this is Marcus Baker from the *Lincolnshire Weekly News*. I heard all about the excitement back in Skegness. The telephone line here in the yurt camp in Barbados is not that good, so I'll get to the point. Listen, since you were at the heart of the solution to the Dancing Hands Mystery, I'd like to commission a series of three feature articles. Miss Timothy will send over a contract tonight. Please sign and return."

I punched my hand in the air, stopped, and said, "Oh, I'll need to find new references."

"No need. I've spoken to your old boss at the *Skegness Telegraph*. A little secret, he's joining the newspaper—keep that under wraps. Just sign the contract, and get it back to the office. We'll need to move fast on this; everything Dancing Hands is hot news."

When I returned to Mrs Lintott's kitchen, Constable Wriggly said, "All charges filed against Grace Rivers are to be dropped—keep that to yourself, for now. She'll get official confirmation next Monday."

"Great news," I said. "And her son, Joey, is doing well. From what Grace told me this morning, he'll be back at school next week, and she starts back at the museum on Monday."

Constable Wriggly placed a hand on his chin. "Mrs Cudlow, what I can't understand is how you got access to the storeroom."

I said, "The tiny room at the back of the archives where I found Jenny's body?"

Constable Wriggly nodded. "According to Fiona Fenchurch, she always kept the door locked, and she was the only person with a key."

I thought about the ghost of Betty Foxley, smiled, then said, "Oh, I don't know. I simply placed my hand on the door handle and pushed. I guess, Fiona forgot to lock it."

Author's Note

Nothing makes me happier than the thought of a reader finishing one of my books.

So, thank you!

If you enjoyed this story, I hope you'll leave a review at the retail website where you purchased it. Reviews help readers like you discover books they will enjoy and help indie authors like me improve our stories.

Until next time,

N.C. Lewis

P.S. As an indie author, I work hard to bring you entertaining cozy mysteries as fast as I can. I've got many more books in the works, and I hope you'll come along for the ride.

Be the First to Know

Want more stories like this? Sign up for my Mystery Newsletter[1] and be the first to know about new book releases, discounts and free books. Or visit: https://www.nclewis.com/newsletter.html

---

1. https://www.subscribepage.com/b8b7j4

ALSO BY N.C. LEWIS - Texas Troubles

Texas Troubles
WANT TO GET AWAY FROM the daily grind? So did Ollie!

Middle aged Professor Ollie Stratford's been hounded by a psycho realtor, outrun by a bunch of grandma's, taken advice from sock puppets, stuck in a brimming toilet bowl, and almost run out of college by a drunken professor. How is that for her first few days in a quiet little Texas town she never wanted to live in?

Thrust into the middle of a murder mystery with a dwindling pile of cash and very few leads Ollie starts digging. Along the way, she teams up with an oddball reporter, a dreadlocks Rastafarian

---

1. https://books2read.com/u/bxqZK6

haired lawyer, a grandma who teaches mixed martial arts, and a stray dog named Bodie. Can she discover the identity of the killer in time or will she end up being the next victim?

If you like cozy mysteries, clever animals, southern charm, and coffee, you'll love Texas Troubles, the first in a fun series of Ollie Stratford Murder Mysteries set in a small Texan Hill Country town, with all its quirky inhabitants.

<u>Grab your copy today!</u>[2]

---

2. https://books2read.com/u/bxqZK6

ALSO BY N.C. LEWIS – Murder in the Bookstore

Murder in the Bookstore
A NEW BUSINESS. A FRESH start. And a murder...

N.C. Lewis

Murder in the Bookstore

An Amy King Cozy Mystery[1]

When Amy King launches her professional staging business on her fiftieth birthday, she has no idea the terrible events that will unfold.

Amy's eager to get things moving and takes on Alan Earl, a well-known Austin antiquarian book dealer.

When he is found dead at his 12th street bookstore, a tangled web of secrets, lies, deceit, and betrayal is exposed.

Quickly, Alan's death turns into something more than she ever anticipated.

---

1. https://books2read.com/u/bP507J

Things get worse when an elder of a local religious cult accuses Amy's new business of unleashing an ancient curse. Now no one's booking and Amy's dream of running a staging business lies on the brink of ruin.

To save her business and protect her reputation, Amy must find out why Alan Earl died and who did it.

But her actions set off a chain of events fueled by jealousy, revenge, violence and hatred.

Amy thought that it would be easy to discover the killer... but she didn't know who else was listening in at the bookstore door.

MURDER IN THE BOOKSTORE is the first in a series of page-turning cozy mysteries set in Austin, the capital of Texas. Pick up this TOTALLY ABSORBING MYSTERY FULL OF STUNNING TWISTS AND TURNS.

<u>Grab your copy today!</u>[2]

---

2. https://books2read.com/u/bP507J

Made in the USA
Coppell, TX
19 July 2020